JOHN CREASEY'S
CRIME COLLECTION 1987

JOHN CREASEY'S CRIME COLLECTION 1987

An Anthology by members of the Crime Writers' Association

edited by

HERBERT HARRIS

LONDON
VICTOR GOLLANCZ LTD
1987

First published in Great Britain 1987
by Victor Gollancz Ltd,
14 Henrietta Street, London WC2E 8QJ

© Victor Gollancz Ltd 1987

British Library Cataloguing in Publication Data
John Creasey's crime collection 1987 : an
   anthology by members of the Crime Writers'
   Association.
   I. Creasey, John, *1908–1973*   II. Harris,
   Herbert, *1911–*
   823'.0872[FS]   PR1309.D4

ISBN 0–575–04100–5

Photoset, printed and bound in Great Britain by
WBC Bristol and Maesteg

CONTENTS

ACKNOWLEDGEMENTS

Acknowledgements are due to *The New Girlfriend & Other Stories* (Hutchinson) for "The Convolvulus Clock" by Ruth Rendell; to *Ellery Queen's Mystery Magazine* for "Curl Up and Dye" by Peter Lovesey, "The Best Chess Player in the World" by Julian Symons, "A Sense of History" by Michael Gilbert, "The Old Haddock" by H. R. F. Keating, and "The Sensory Deprivation Tank" by Celia Fremlin; to *Espionage Magazine* (USA) for "The Finger of Suspicion" by Tony Wilmot; to *Pascoe's Ghost* (Collins) for "Exit Line" by Reginald Hill; to the *Daily Mail* (London) for "Be Lucky" by Allan Prior; to *London Mystery Selection* for "The Call of the Running Tide" by Judy Chard; to *Crime Wave* (Collins) for "Murder à la Mode" by Richard Grayson; to *New Black Mask Quarterly* (USA) for "Remember Mrs Fitz" by George Sims. Original stories in this anthology are "House Poison" by Antonia Fraser, "The Notif" by Madelaine Duke, "Death at the Barbecue" by Herbert Harris, and "Cast for Murder" by Kenneth Benton.

INTRODUCTION

I think I may claim to have come of age with this edition of *John Creasey's Crime Collection*, for it is the twenty-first short-story anthology I have compiled, using stories by members of the Crime Writers' Association and linked with the name of the late John Creasey, who founded the Association in 1953.

The forerunner of this series was *John Creasey's Mystery Bedside Book*, edited by John himself for the first six years, then passed to me for its conversion into a CWA anthology, which it has been since 1966. It now enjoys, I believe, a sound reputation for collecting from a variety of sources some of the outstanding work produced in this highly specialized genre.

In the last volume of the "Bedside Book" which Creasey edited he wrote: "Because of the dwindling number of magazines which use the short story, few younger writers have the opportunity of learning their craft professionally, and many of today's best short stories are the byline (a most apt American word) of authors already well-known in other spheres. There remains a small but stubborn group of authors who write short stories (obviously) for love. It certainly cannot be for the money."

Now, two decades later, little has changed. Few markets exist for the short story, and the anthologies, such as this one, have become the principal outlet for those who write short stories for love.

Surprisingly few of our well-known novelists can write short stories successfully, but those who do often produce some of their most brilliant work in the shorter length, perhaps *because* they are writing for love. Some of it, I hope, the reader will find in this year's Collection.

HERBERT HARRIS

THE CONVOLVULUS CLOCK

Ruth Rendell

"Is that your own hair, dear?"

Sibyl only laughed. She made a roguish face.

"I didn't think it could be," said Trixie. "It looks so thick."

"A woman came up to me in the street the other day," said Sibyl, "and asked me where I had my hair set. I just looked at her. I gave a tiny little tip to my wig like this. You should have seen her face."

She gave another roar of laughter. Trixie smiled austerely. She had come to stay with Sibyl for a week and this was her first evening. Sibyl had bought a cottage in Devonshire. It was two years since Trixie had seen Sibyl and she could detect signs of deterioration. What a pity that was! Sibyl enquired after the welfare of the friends they had in common. How was Mivvy? Did Trixie see anything of the Fishers? How was Poppy?

"Poppy is beginning to go a bit funny," said Trixie.

"How do you mean, 'funny'?"

"You know. Funny. Not quite *compos mentis* any more."

Sibyl of all people ought to know what going funny meant, thought Trixie.

"We're none of us getting any younger," said Sibyl, laughing.

Trixie didn't sleep very well. She got up at five and had her bath so as to leave the bathroom clear for Sibyl. At seven she took Sibyl a cup of tea. She gave a little scream and nearly dropped the tray.

"Oh my conscience! I'm sorry, dear, but I thought that was a squirrel on your chest of drawers. I thought it must have come in through the window."

"What on earth was that noise in the middle of the night?"

When Sibyl wasn't laughing she could be downright peevish. She looked a hundred without her wig. "It woke me up; I thought the tank was overflowing."

"The middle of the night! I like that. The sun had been up a good hour, I'm sure. I was just having my bath so as not to be a nuisance."

They went out in Sibyl's car. They had lunch in Dawlish and tea in Exmouth. The following day they went out early and drove across Dartmoor. When they got back there was a letter on the mat for Trixie from Mivvy, though Trixie had only been away two days. On Friday Sibyl said they would stay at home and have a potter about the village. The church was famous, the Manor House gardens were open to the public and there was an interesting small gallery where an exhibition was on. She started to get the car out but Trixie said why couldn't they walk. It could hardly be more than a mile. Sibyl said it was just under two miles but she agreed to walk if Trixie really wanted to. Her knee hadn't been troubling her quite so much lately.

"The gallery is called Artifacts," said Sibyl. "It's run by a very nice young couple."

"A husband and wife team?" asked Trixie, very modern.

"Jimmy and Judy they're called. I don't think they are actually married."

"Oh my conscience, Sibyl, how can one be 'actually' married? Surely one is either married or not?" Trixie herself had been married once, long ago, for a short time. Sibyl had never been married and neither had Mivvy or Poppy. Trixie thought that might have something to do with their going funny. "Thankfully, I'm broad-minded. I shan't say anything. I think I can see a seat ahead in that bus shelter. Would you like a little sit-down before we go on?"

Sibyl got her breath back and they walked on more slowly. The road passed between high hedges on high banks dense with wild flowers. It crossed a stream by a hump-backed bridge where the clear brown shallow water rippled over a bed of stones. The church appeared with granite nave and tower, standing on an eminence and approached, Sibyl said, by fifty-three steps. Perhaps they should go to Artifacts first?

The gallery was housed in an ancient building with bow windows and a front door set under a Georgian portico. When the door was pushed open a bell tinkled to summon Jimmy or Judy. This morning, however, they needed no summoning for both were in the first room, Judy dusting the dolls' house and Jimmy doing something to the ceiling spotlights. Sibyl introduced Trixie to them and Trixie was very gracious towards Judy, making no difference in her manner than she would have if the young woman had been properly married and worn a wedding ring.

Trixie was agreeably surprised by the objects in the exhibition and by the items Jimmy and Judy had for sale. She had not expected such a high standard. What she admired most particularly were the small pictures of domestic interiors done in embroidery, the patchwork quilts and the blown glass vases in colours of mother-of-pearl and butterfly wings. What she liked best of all and wanted to have was a clock.

There were four of these clocks, all different. The cases were ceramic, plain and smooth or made in a trellis work, glazed in blues and greens, painted with flowers or the moon and stars, each incorporating a gilt-rimmed face and quartz movement. Trixie's favourite was blue with a green trellis over the blue, a convolvulus plant with green leaves and pale pink trumpet flowers climbing the trellis and a gilt rim round the face of the clock which had hands of gilt and blue. The convolvulus reminded her of the pattern on her best china tea-service. All the clocks had price cards beside them and red discs stuck to the cards.

"I should like to buy this clock," Trixie said to Judy.

"I'm terribly sorry but it's sold."

"Sold?"

"All the clocks were sold at the private view. Roland Elm's work is tremendously popular. He can't make enough of these clocks and he refuses to take orders."

"I still don't understand why I can't buy this one," said Trixie. "This is a shop, isn't it?"

Sibyl had put on her peevish look. "You can see the red sticker, can't you? You know what that means."

"I know what it means at the Royal Academy but hardly here surely."

"I really do wish I could sell it to you," said Judy, "but I can't."

Trixie lifted her shoulders. She was very disappointed and wished she hadn't come. She had been going to buy Sibyl a pear carved from polished pear-wood but now she thought better of it. The church also was a let-down, dark, poky and smelling of mould.

"Things have come to a pretty pass when shopkeepers won't sell their goods to you because they're upset by your manner."

"Judy wasn't upset by your manner," said Sibyl, puffing. "It's more than her reputation is worth to sell you something she's already sold."

"Reputation! I like that."

"I mean reputation as a gallery owner. Artifacts is quite highly regarded round here."

"You would have thought she and her—well, partner, would be glad of sixty-two pounds. I don't suppose they have two halfpennies to bless themselves with."

What Sibyl would have thought was never known for she was too out of breath to utter a word and when they got home had to lie down. Next morning another letter came from Mivvy.

"Nothing to say for herself of course," said Trixie at breakfast. "Practically a carbon copy of Thursday's. She's going very funny. Do you know she told me sometimes she writes fifty letters in a week? God bless your pocket, I said. It's fortunate you can afford it."

They went to Princetown in Sibyl's car and Widecombe-in-the-Moor. Trixie sent postcards to Mivvy, Poppy, the Fishers and the woman who came in to clean and water the plants in the greenhouse. She would have to buy some sort of present for Sibyl before she left. A plant would have done, only Sibyl didn't like gardening. They went to a bird sanctuary and looked at some standing stones of great antiquity. Trixie was going home on Tuesday afternoon. On Tuesday morning another letter arrived from Mivvy all about the Fishers going to see the Queen Mother open a new arts centre in Leighton Buzzard. The Fishers were crazy about the Queen Mother, watched for her engagements in advance and went wherever she went within a radius of 150 miles in order just to catch a glimpse of her. Once they had been at the front of the crowd and the Queen Mother had shaken hands with Dorothy Fisher.

"We're none of us getting any younger," said Sibyl, giggling.

"Well, my conscience, I know one thing," said Trixie. "The days have simply flown past while I've been here."

"I'm glad you've enjoyed yourself."

"Oh, I have, dear, only it would please me to see you a little less frail."

Trixie walked to the village on her own. Since she couldn't think of anything else she was going to have to buy the pear-wood for Sibyl. It was a warm sunny morning, one of the best days she'd had, and the front door of Artifacts stood open to the street. The exhibition was still on and the clocks (and their red "sold" discs) still there. A shaft of sunlight streamed across the patchwork quilts on to the Georgian dolls' house. There was no sign of Jimmy and Judy. The gallery was empty but for herself.

Trixie closed the door and opened it to make the bell ring. She picked up one of the pear-wood pears and held it out in front of her on the palm of her hand. She held it at arm's length the way she did when she had helped herself to an item in the supermarket just so that there couldn't be the slightest question of anyone suspecting her of shoplifting. No one came. Trixie climbed the stairs, holding the pear-wood pear out in front of her and clearing her throat to attract attention. There was no one upstairs. A blue Persian cat lay sleeping on a shelf between a ginger jar and a mug with an owl on it. Trixie descended. She closed the front door and opened it to make the bell ring. Jimmy and Judy must be a heedless pair, she thought. Anyone could walk in here and steal the lot.

Of course she could just take the pear-wood pear and leave a five-pound note to pay for it. It cost four pounds seventy-five. Why should she make Jimmy and Judy a present of twenty-five pence just because they were too idle to serve her? Then she remembered that when she had been here with Sibyl a door at the end of the passage had been open and through that door one could see the garden where there was a display of terracotta pots. It was probable Jimmy and Judy were out there, showing the pots to a customer.

Trixie went through the second room and down the passage.

The door to the garden was just ajar and she pushed it open. On the lawn, in a cane chair, Judy lay fast asleep. A ledger had fallen off her lap and lay on the grass alongside a heap of books. Guides to the management of tax they were; also some which looked like the gallery account books. It reminded Trixie of Poppy who was always falling asleep in the daytime, most embarrassingly sometimes, at the table or even while waiting for a bus. Judy had fallen asleep over her book-keeping. Trixie coughed. She said "Excuse me" very loudly and repeated it, but Judy didn't stir.

What a way to run a business! It would serve them right if someone walked in and cleared their shop. It would teach them a lesson. Trixie pulled the door closed behind her. She found herself tiptoeing as she walked back along the passage and through the second room. In the first room she took the ceramic clock with the convolvulus on it off the shelf and put it into her bag and she took the card too with the red sticker on it so as not to attract attention to the clock's absence. The pear-wood she replaced among the other carved fruit.

The street outside seemed deserted. Trixie's heart was beating rather fast. She went across the road into the little newsagent's and gift shop and bought Sibyl a tea-cloth with a map of Devonshire on it. At the door, as she was coming out again, she saw Jimmy coming along the street towards the gallery with a bag of groceries under one arm and two pints of milk in the other. Trixie stayed where she was until he had gone into Artifacts.

She didn't much fancy the walk back but there was no help for it. When she got to the bridge over the stream she heard hooves behind her and for a second or two had a feeling she was pursued by men on horseback but it was only a girl who passed her, riding a fat white pony. Sibyl laughed when she saw the tea-cloth and said it was a funny thing to give someone who *lived* in Devonshire. Trixie felt nervous and couldn't eat her lunch. Jimmy and Judy would have missed the clock by now and the newsagent would have remembered a furtive-looking woman skulking in his doorway and described her to them and soon the police would come. If only Sibyl would hurry with the car! She moved so slowly time had no meaning for her. At this rate Trixie wouldn't even catch her train at Exeter.

She did catch it—just. Sibyl's car had been followed for several miles of the way by police in a Rover with a blue lamp on top and Trixie's heart had been in her mouth. Why had she done it? What had possessed her to take something she hadn't paid for, she who when shopping in supermarkets held seventeen-pence pots of yoghurt at arm's length?

Now she was safely in the train rushing towards Paddington she began to see things in a different light. She would have paid for that clock if they had let her. What did she expect if they refused to sell things they had on sale? And what *could* they expect if they went to sleep leaving their shop unattended? For a few moments she had a nasty little qualm that the police might be waiting for her outside her own door but they weren't. Inside all was as it should be, all was as she had left it except that Poppy had put a pint of milk in the fridge and someone had arranged dahlias in a vase—not Poppy, she wouldn't know a dahlia from a runner bean.

That would be just the place for the clock, on the wall bracket where at present stood a photograph of herself and Dorothy Fisher at Broadstairs in 1949. Trixie put the photograph away in a drawer and the clock where the photograph had been. It looked nice. It transformed a rather dull corner of the room. Trixie put one of the cups from her tea-service beside it and it was amazing how well they matched.

Mivvy came round first thing in the morning. Before letting her in Trixie quickly snatched the clock off the shelf and thrust it inside the drawer with the photograph. It seemed so *exposed* up there; it seemed to tell its history in every tiny tick.

"How did you find Sibyl?"

Trixie wanted to say, I went in the train to Exeter and got out at the station and there was Sibyl waiting for me in her car . . . Only if you started mocking poor Mivvy where would you end? "Very frail, dear. I thought she was going a bit funny."

"I must drop her a line."

Mivvy always spoke as if her letters held curative properties. Receiving one of them would set you up for the winter. After she had gone Trixie considered replacing the clock on the shelf but thought better of it. Let it stay in the drawer for a bit. She had read of South American millionaires who have Old Masters stolen for them which they can never show but are obliged, for fear of discovery, to keep hidden away for ever in dark vaults.

Just before Christmas a letter came from Sibyl. They always sent each other Christmas letters. As Trixie said, if you can't get around to writing the rest of the year, at least you can at Christmas. Mivvy wrote hundreds. Sibyl didn't mention the theft of the clock or indeed mention the gallery at all. Trixie wondered why not. The clock was still in the drawer. Sometimes she lay awake in the night thinking about it, fancying she could hear its tick through the solid mahogany of the drawer, through the ceiling and the bedroom floorboards.

It was curious how she had taken a dislike to the convolvulus tea-service. One day she found herself wrapping it in tissue paper and putting it away in the cupboard under the stairs. She took down all the trellis work round the front door and put up wires for the clematis instead. In March she wrote to Sibyl to enquire if there was a new exhibition on at Artifacts. Sibyl didn't answer for weeks. When she did she told Trixie that months and months back one of those ceramic clocks had been stolen from the gallery and a few days later an embroidered picture had also gone and furniture out of the dolls' house. Hadn't Sibyl mentioned it before? She thought she had but she was getting so forgetful these days.

Trixie took the clock out of the drawer and put it on the shelf. Because she knew she couldn't be found out she began to feel she hadn't done anything wrong. The Fishers were bringing Poppy round for a cup of tea. Trixie started unpacking the convolvulus tea-service. She lost her nerve when she heard Gordon Fisher's car door slam and she put the clock away again. If she were caught now she might get blamed for the theft of the picture and the dolls' house furniture as well. They would say she had sold those things and how could she prove she hadn't?

Poppy fell asleep half-way through her second buttered scone. "She gets funnier every time I see her," Trixie said. "Sad really. Sibyl's breaking up too. She'll forget her own name next. You should see her letters. I'll just show you the last one." She remembered she couldn't do that, it wouldn't be wise, so she had to pretend she'd mislaid it.

"Will you be going down there again this year, dear?" said Dorothy.

"Oh, I expect so. You know how it is, you get to the stage of thinking it may be the last time."

Poppy woke up with a snort, said she hadn't been asleep and finished her scone.

Gordon asked Trixie, "Would you like to come with us and see Her Majesty open the new leisure complex in Rayleigh on Monday?"

Trixie declined. The Fishers went off to do their shopping, leaving Poppy behind. She was asleep again. She slept till six and waking, asked Trixie if she had put something in her tea. It was most unusual, she said, for her to nod off like that. Trixie walked her back to the bus stop because the traffic whipped along there so fast you had to have your wits about you and drivers didn't respect zebra crossings the way they used to. Trixie marched across on the stripes, confident as a lollipop lady but without the lollipop, taking her life in her hands instead.

She wrote to Sibyl that she would come to Devonshire at the end of July, thinking that while there it might be best to make some excuse to avoid going near Artifacts. The clock was still in the drawer but wrapped up now in a piece of old flannel. Trixie had taken a dislike to seeing the colour of it each time she opened the drawer. She had a summer dress that colour and she wondered why she had ever bought it, it didn't flatter her, whatever it might do for the Queen Mother. Dorothy could have it for her next jumble sale.

Walking back from posting a letter, Mivvy fell over and broke her ankle. It was weeks getting back to normal. Well, you had to face it, it was never going to be *normal*. You wouldn't be exaggerating, Trixie wrote to Sibyl, if you said that obsession of hers for writing letters had crippled her for life. Sibyl wrote back to say she was looking forward to the last week of July and what did Trixie think had happened? They had caught the thief of the pieces from Artifacts trying to sell the picture to a dealer in Plymouth. He had said in court he hadn't taken the clock but you could imagine how much credence the magistrate placed on that!

Trixie unwrapped the clock and put it on the shelf. Next day she got the china out. She wondered why she had been so precipitate in pulling all that trellis off the wall; it looked a lot better than strands of wire on metal hooks. Mivvy came round in a taxi, hobbling up the path on two sticks, refusing the offer of the taxi driver's arm.

"You'll be off to Sibyl's in a day or two, will you, dear?"

Trixie didn't know how many times she had told her not till Monday week. She was waiting for Mivvy to notice the clock but at this rate she was going to have to wait till Christmas.

"What do you think of my clock?"

"What, up there? Isn't that your Wedgwood coffee-pot, dear?"

Trixie had to get it down. She thrust it under Mivvy's nose and started explaining what it was.

But Mivvy knew already. "Of course I know it's a clock, dear. It's not the first time I've seen one of these. Oh my goodness, no. The young man who makes these, he's a friend of my nephew Tony, they were at art school together. Let me see, what's his name? It will come to me in a minute. A tree, isn't it? Oak? Ash? Peter Oak? No, Elm is his name. Something Elm. Roland Elm."

Trixie said nothing. The glazed surface of the clock felt very cold against the skin of her hands.

"He never makes them to order, you know. He just makes a limited number for a few selected galleries. Tony told me that. Where did you get yours, I wonder?"

Trixie said nothing. There was worse coming and she waited for it.

"Not around here, I'm sure. I know there are only two or three places in the country they go to. It will come to me in a minute. I shall be writing to Tony tomorrow and I'll mention about you having one of Richard's—no, I mean Raymond's, that is, Roland's, clocks. I always write to him on Tuesdays. Tuesday is his day. I'll mention you've got one with bindweed on it. They're all different, you know. He never makes two alike."

"It's convolvulus, not bindweed," said Trixie. "I'd rather you didn't write to Tony about it if you don't mind."

"Oh, but I'd like to mention it, dear. Whyever not? I won't mention your name if you don't want me to. I'll just say that lady who goes down to stay with Auntie Sibyl in Devonshire."

Trixie said she would walk with Mivvy up to the High Street. It was hopeless trying to get a taxi outside here. She fetched Mivvy's two sticks.

"You take my arm and I'll hold your other stick."

The traffic whipped along over the zebra crossing. You were at the mercy of those drivers, Trixie said, it was a matter of waiting till they condescended to stop.

"Don't you set foot on those stripes till they stop," she said to Mivvy.

. Mivvy didn't so the cars didn't stop. A container lorry, a juggernaut, came thundering along, but a good way off still. Trixie thought it was going much too fast.

"Now if we're quick," she said. "Run for it!"

Startled by the urgency in her voice, Mivvy obeyed, or tried to obey as Trixie dropped her arm and gave her a little push forward. The lorry's brakes screamed like people being tortured and Trixie jumped back, screaming herself, covering her face with her hands so as not to see Mivvy under those giant wheels.

Dorothy Fisher said she quite understood Trixie would still want to go to Sibyl's for her holiday. It was the best thing in the world for her, a rest, a complete change, a chance to forget. Trixie went down by train on the day after the funeral. She had the clock in her bag with her, wrapped first in tissue paper and then in her sky-blue dress. The first opportunity that offered itself she would take the clock back to Artifacts and replace it on the shelf she had taken it from. This shouldn't be too difficult. The clock was a dangerous possession, she could see that, like one of those notorious diamonds that carry a curse with them. Pretty though it was, it was an *unlucky* clock that had involved her in trouble from the time she had first taken it.

There was no question of walking to Artifacts this time. Sibyl was too frail for that. She had gone downhill a lot since last year and symptomatic of her deterioration was her exchange of the grey wig for a lilac-blue one. They went in the car though Trixie was by no means sure Sibyl was safe at the wheel.

As soon as they walked into the gallery Trixie saw that she had no hope of replacing the clock without being spotted. There was a desk in the first room now with a plump smiling lady sitting at it who Sibyl said was Judy's mother. Trixie thought that amazing—a mother not minding her daughter cohabiting with a man she wasn't married to. Living with a daughter living in sin, you might put it. Jimmy was in the second room, up on a ladder doing something to the window catch.

"They're having upstairs remodelled," said Sibyl. "You can't go up there." And when Trixie tried to make her way towards the garden door, "You don't want to be had up for trespassing, do you?" She winked at Judy's mother. "We're none of us getting any younger when all's said and done, are we?"

They went back to Sibyl's, the clock still in Trixie's bag. It seemed to have grown heavier. She could hear it ticking through the leather and the folds of the sky-blue dress. In the afternoon when Sibyl lay down on the sofa for her rest, the lilac wig stuck on top of a Poole pottery vase, Trixie went out for a walk, taking the clock with her. She came to the hump-backed bridge over the stream where the water was very low, for it had been a dry summer. She unwrapped the clock and dropped it over the parapet into the water. It cracked but the trellis work and the convolvulus remained intact and the movement continued to move and to tick as well for all Trixie knew. The blue and green, the pink flowers and the gilt, gleamed through the water like some exotic iridescent shell.

Trixie went down the bank. She took off her shoes and waded into the water. It was surprisingly cold. She picked up a large flat stone and beat at the face of the clock with it. She beat with unrestrained fury, gasping and grunting at each blow. The green trellis and the blue sky, the glass face and the pink flowers, all shattered. But they were still there, bright jewel-like shards, for all to see who came this way across the bridge.

Squatting down, Trixie scooped up handfuls of pebbles and buried the pieces of clock under them. With her nails she dug a pit in the bed of the stream and pushed the coloured fragments into it, covering them with more pebbles. Her hands were bleeding, her knees were bruised and her dress was wet. In spite of her efforts the bed of the stream was still spread with ceramic chips and broken glass and pieces of gilt metal. Trixie began to sob and crawl from side to side of the stream, ploughing her hands through the blue and green and gold gravel, and it was there that one of

Sibyl's neighbours found her as he was driving home over the bridge.

He lifted her up and carried her to his car.

"Tick-tock," said Trixie. "Tick-tock. Convolvulus clock."

CURL UP AND DYE

Peter Lovesey

"HOW WOULD YOU like it today, sir? Amazing how fast it grows, isn't it? A quick trim all round, perhaps, just to tidy you up? You wouldn't want too much off. Not like the old days. This dates me, I know, but I go back to the wartime, shearing the rookies as they joined up. RAF basic training camp. I was the next in line after the recruitment interview and the medical. If they got as far as me, there was definitely no escape. Fifteen heads an hour, I cut in those days. It was the war effort, you see. All done with scissors and hand-clippers. We weren't on electric. Yet I swear I never drew blood, and if I did I had my styptic pencil ready.

"You don't mind me talking as I work? I told them when I offered myself for this, don't expect me to do it in silence. I'm a compulsive talker, and none of your regulations are going to stop me. I shall fraternize. People don't want a silent barber, do they? Talking is part of the experience. I've had customers—clients, I ought to call them these days—who tell me they come for the conversation. It's a bit one-way with me, I know, but you'd be surprised how much you can learn by listening. Politics, sport, last night's television, travel. I haven't actually been abroad myself, but the wife is an authority. You know the way some women sit up in bed reading those romantic novels? Well, my Brenda reads travel brochures. She has them stacked by the bed. Hundreds. She can tell you the temperature in Torremolinos, or how to approach an African bull elephant or haggle with a gondolier. I'm always learning something new from Brenda. She's sixty-five and never been further than Clacton, but you could take her anywhere. The place she really wants to see is China. I say to her wouldn't you settle for the Costa Brava and a Chinese take-away, but no, she's set her heart on seeing the Great Wall and the pandas. So I saved up for years, and last summer, we almost got there. It makes me hopping mad to think about it. I booked the China tour as a surprise. Paid the deposit without letting her know. The first Brenda knew of it was when I told her casually she'd be needing some injections. She was on to it in a flash. I've never seen her so excited. Then what do you think happened? A bolt from the blue. Disaster.

"How does the front look to you, sir? A little more to come off, would you say? We could train it across, or let it fall over the forehead in the modern style. If you ask me, it wants another half-inch off. All right?

"My disaster. You just wouldn't believe what happened. I must tell you that I'd worked in the same shop in Battersea since I was demobbed in 1945. A real, old-fashioned barber's shop with the striped pole outside, and three adjustable leather chairs, the sort with head-rests. A bench behind, where the customers waited and read *Picture Post* and *Everybody's*. The smell of Brylcreem in the air. This is before your time, sir. Two assistants and a boy to do the sweeping. Scores of regular customers. Men I'd known since their mothers brought them in as nippers and perched them on a piece of wood across the arms of the chair. I had the monopoly, you see. The only barber in Battersea High Street. There was Sally Anne's, the ladies' salon, across the street, and between us we had the hair-cutting business wrapped up. Not that I took advantage, mind. I always charged the going rate. There aren't many overheads in barbering, if you'll excuse the pun. If people wanted to be generous with tips, that was another thing.

"Old Smithy, my boss, retired in 1962, and I bought the business. Put in some nice chrome fittings and a few more electric points, but kept the character of the establishment, if you know what I mean. I was proud of what I'd achieved. Barbering is an honourable trade, mentioned more than once in Shakespeare. 'I must to the barber's, mounsieur; for methinks I am marvellous hairy about the face.' *A Midsummer Night's Dream*. You didn't take me for a connoisseur of the stage, did you? Appearances can be deceptive. Take yourself, for example. No offence, but who'd expect to find a man of class like you in a place like this?

"To come back to last year, I was standing by the shop window in a quiet moment between customers one morning last July, when I noticed something going on across the road. Well, not exactly going on. *Coming off* is what I ought to say, and what was coming off was the sign over Sally Anne's salon. Nobody had told me the place was changing hands, but in my time that particular business has been bought and sold seven times over. There isn't the continuity in ladies' hairdressing that you find in the gents' side of the business.

"Forward slightly, if you would, sir. Perfect.

"In the course of that day and the next, I kept an eye on the progress of the workmen. The entire shop-front was taken out and tarted up. Smoked glass with white gloves and top hats painted on it. A tiled surround. Even a ruddy door that opened automatically. A trifle over the top for Battersea, I thought, but maybe I'm old-fashioned. The real shock was yet to come.

"I don't have to tell you that ladies' hairdressing is a growth industry—if you'll pardon another pun. Anyone with half an eye can see that new salons have opened all over the country in the last ten years. I should think they've trebled in number. It's cut-throat competition. Look at some of the names they dream up. You've got to laugh. The Friendly Wave. Beyond the Fringe. How they think of them, I can't imagine. There's a salon down Bermondsey way called Shear Genius. But the one that really creases me is Curl Up and Dye. How about that?

"Quite still, sir. Wouldn't want to nick your ear, would I?

"This one across the street from me was called Toppers. Don't stop me now, will you? I'd like to finish the story if you've got the time, and I reckon you have. As I was saying, I saw the sign go up over the shop. Watched the fellows screwing it in place. Very up-market lettering, it was. Black on silver, all glittering, like. Fair enough, I thought, Toppers might have more going for it than Sally Anne's. Best of luck. I hope for your sakes the ladies of Battersea go for it. Then I happened to notice there was another word under it, in smaller letters. I had to step outside my shop to see it properly. It was 'Unisex'.

"I tell you, I practically blew a gasket when I saw it. Unisex. They were moving in on my trade. Right there across the street from me, without so much as a by-your-leave, chum. After almost forty years. I marched across and asked them just what the hell was going on. The young blokes said the sign was going on, and that was all they knew about it. They were just the shop outfitters. If I had any complaints, I'd better address them to the management when the shop opened on Monday.

"Management! Do you know who they put in charge of that shop? Some young girl of seventeen. Maybe eighteen. No older. She looked as if she was taking a day off school. She had five others working with her. The only way of telling who was in charge was that this one chewed gum. Naturally, she wasn't the owner. She couldn't tell me who was. She took her instructions from a fellow called Stan who was coming to collect the takings at the end of the day. I told her I'd like a word with him, but of course I got nowhere. Stan sensed some aggro, and he wasn't staying to cop it.

"I tried several times to catch up with him, and then I thought, blow me, why bother? I'll take it up with the Chamber of Commerce. So I did. And what good did it do? Sweet FA. 'We all have to face competition, you know,' they told me. 'It's a free market. You've had a good run. The day of the one-sex salon is numbered. Have you thought of expanding into ladies' hairdressing?' I won't tell you what I answered to that. No disrespect, but I'm a barber and I'll die a barber, not a blinking teazy-weezy.

"So there was no support from that quarter. It was pretty obvious that I just had to get on, or get out. My prices were competitive, and I did a good job. Nothing fancy, but who wants his hair shampooed and dried with a blower? All right, I lost a few of my younger customers. I expected to. If you ask me, it wasn't the styling they went for, it was the chance to chat up the talent over there.

"After a couple of months, I was feeling more happy about it. I won't say I didn't feel the draught a bit, but I told myself it was worth sitting it out to see the competition off. I was kidding myself.

"One evening at six-thirty, when the 'closed' notice is up and I'm locking up, some big fellow steps out of a Cortina and approaches me. 'Sorry,' I tell him, 'I'm closing,' but I can see at a glance that he doesn't actually need a haircut. He's as bald as a baby. He says, 'Smart thinking, squire. I can see you've got it all weighed up.' I say, 'What do you mean?' and he says, 'Like you just said, you're closing. Congratulations on your retirement. Shall we say next Saturday?' He steps past me into the shop and says, 'Not a bad place. A bit run down, but in a good position. You ought to get a fair price.' I don't like the sound of this at all, but I manage to smile, and say, 'I think you're misinformed. I've got no intention of retiring.' To which he says in a low voice, 'It's been decided. Better put up a notice tomorrow. Let your regular customers know. And call in at the agent's by the station. They'll soon flog this for you.' I say, 'Who sent you?' But he won't tell me, so I say, 'What if I don't want to sell?' He just gives a shrug and says, 'It isn't a question of what you want, squire.' Then he walks out, gets into his car and drives away. I've never seen him since.

"I suppose you're wondering what I did about it. Can't expect you to have heard about my little drama. I ignored it. Carried on as usual. Saturday came and nothing happened. Brenda wasn't feeling too good on Sunday. She'd just had her injections for the China trip. So we stayed in. No, that's a lie. I slipped out to the pub for a pint at lunch-time and met Humphrey Lawson, the fellow who runs the record shop next door to mine. He asked me something about the alterations I was having done to the shop. I said, 'What alterations?' He told me he'd been past the back of the shops on his way to church and seen one of those cement-mixing lorries backing up towards my place. I said it must have been a mistake. I wasn't having any work done.

"I forgot about it until Monday morning. Turned up at the shop and couldn't open the door. There was a two-foot layer of rock-hard concrete right through the shop and the room behind. That's what the bastards did to my business. Forced open a window at the back and spread a ton of wet cement across the floor. I had to get the fire brigade to smash through the door, and then it was like stepping on to a platform. My head was touching the ceiling. All my stuff was ruined. Chairs, cupboards, plumbing, even the plate glass windows. I was ruined. I mean, I faced a massive bill just to get the place into a fit state to sell to someone else.

"We cancelled the China trip and gave up the shop. Brenda was heart-broken. She'll never get that holiday now. The shop became a laundrette. My customers had to change the habits of a lifetime. It was a cut-and-blow-dry at Toppers for twice the price after that.

All by appointment only and how about some of our special conditioner for sixty pence extra? When I found out what had happened, and why, I felt sick to the back teeth. It wasn't just my business that folded. This was happening all over London. One of the East End mobs had set up a chain of unisex hairdressers. They went under all sorts of fancy names, but the form was the same: move into a prime position in the high street, tart up the shop-front, hire a handful of teenage girls for peanuts and put the frighteners on the competition. Anyone who didn't agree to close got a weekend visit like mine.

"How are we doing, sir? I'll just run the razor up the back of your neck. This is one of the few things I managed to save from the shop. This, and my scissors and comb and the old-fashioned cut-throat I use for trimming the sideboards. That's a service you wouldn't get in those unisex salons. A cut-throat razor gives an unbeatable finish. Funny, I've become very possessive about my equipment since the shop went. I carry everything in this case. Won't let it out of my sight.

"You're probably wondering what all this did to my life. It's not *my* life I'm bothered about, sir. I had a good run. I don't care what happens to me. It was Brenda who took the biggest knock. She really wanted that trip to China. You've got to understand that it was the great ambition of her life. She's not the same person at all now. Shattered. No interest in anything. Just sits and stares all day. She's been to doctors, psychiatrists . . . She'd be better off in a mental ward, poor duck.

"As for me, I've adjusted pretty well. There's always work for a barber, and if the customers can't come to you, the obvious thing is to go to them. I thought of hospital work at first, but there aren't the openings that you'd think. Round here, it's all carved up between a couple of barbers who were forced out of business before I lost mine.

"You know, there are ex-barbers all over London who were clobbered by the same mob. All right, the law caught up with the bully-boys eventually. But we lost our livelihoods. We can't start up again. Most of us haven't got the capital.

"Don't ever talk to me about justice. What happened when the case came to court? Toppers was forced to close, and now there isn't a barber in Battersea High Street. My old customers have a two-mile bus ride if they want a haircut. Crazy.

"Anyway, not to be beaten, I applied to the prison service. I thought prisoners need haircuts the same as anyone else, and I was right. They took me on. So here I am. I've built it up to four days a week in the last six months. That's three prisons, including this one. I don't mind the work. No tips, of course. They expect *me* to bring in cigarettes. No, don't ask me sir. I've none left today.

"You have to be responsible working in prison, mind. It's all a matter of trust. They used to search me as I came through the gate, but they never found anything except a packet of fags which I said was my own, and my barbering implements. I'd be a fool to try anything, wouldn't I? I mean, trying to smuggle in a gun or drugs, or something. I find the vast majority of you prisoners very co-operative, as a matter of fact. Given a chance—and I am a compulsive talker, I admit—most prisoners talk quite freely to me. It's a sort of escape, I suppose, spending twenty minutes with a barber. Like a link with the world outside.

"That's what I tell myself. I'm performing a social service. I keep it as civilized as conditions allow. Just you and me in here and the screw outside. I said at the outset I'll take one man at a time. I don't want anyone behind my back, not when there's scissors in my hand. The next man comes in when I'm ready, and not before.

"Have a squint in the mirror, now, and see what you think. Nice job? And the back? Good. Don't get up, sir. I want to tidy you up with my cut-throat. Sideboards are just a little ragged, aren't they? A man like you is used to being decently turned out. Oh, yes, I know a bit about you, sir. Quite a lot. Picked it up here and there from my clients in the prisons. I know what you're in for. Six months, isn't it, for demanding money with menaces?

"Took me a while to track you down. I mean, I didn't know your face, and you wouldn't know me. I don't suppose you even heard of me, a big shot like yourself. The man who came to my shop that Saturday night was just one of your bully-boys, one of dozens. You wouldn't know who he was if I asked you now. But I wasn't interested in him. I wanted to find the man who gave the orders. Barbering has its uses. Snip-snip. Snippets of information. I can listen, as well as talk. You pleaded guilty, shopped a few of your mates, and the police didn't press the charges of violence that would have put you away for much longer.

"What I say is that prison isn't bad enough for the likes of you, ruining people's lives. Easy, sir. I don't want to strangle you. That wouldn't be a barber's way. I'm just pulling the strings of the cape nice and tight to get a grip. You won't feel much. I sharpened it specially this morning. Like I said, it gives an unbeatable finish."

THE BEST CHESS PLAYER IN THE WORLD

Julian Symons

"ALL I ASK is value for money," George Bernard Shaw said.

The man on the other side of the desk, whose name was Roberts, shuffled his feet and looked miserable.

Shaw had been given those first names by his parents, because it was on the night of a visit to *Arms and the Man* that he had been conceived. Others might have flinched from the names, but he had accepted them even at school, and for years now had taken pleasure in using the full name, or for preference the magic initials. He regarded himself as a disciple of the original George Bernard Shaw, who in his eyes had not been a visionary socialist but a ruthless realist, fighting battles in his dealings with theatre producers, publishers, women, battles which he always won. The original Shaw had been, as he saw it, a man with cranky ideas which he cleverly exploited in plays to make himself a lot of money. In life, however, he had been a logical man, and the later GBS prided himself on being logical too.

He was twenty-five when he inherited from his father a small family printing firm and a couple of weekly local papers. The local papers were now a flourishing chain of thirty, that covered the Midlands and extended up into Yorkshire and Lancashire. The printing works had enlarged with the papers.

Success had not been achieved without some difficulties, as is the way of life. There had been problems with wholesalers in some areas, people who complained that GBS gave much poorer terms than his competitors, and so refused to stock his papers. These wholesalers found their vans damaged through slashed tyres, sand in the tank, and other means. Their warehouses also suffered burglaries, in which stock was damaged or destroyed. Such difficulties ceased when they handled, and pushed, GBS papers.

Then there were union problems at the works. GBS always refused to employ union members, and the local branches threatened to black him. The two union secretaries who had led the blacking movement were badly beaten up, one sustaining several broken ribs and the other a hip injury that left him permanently lame. Half a dozen other militants suffered similar, although less severe attacks, and eventually GBS's firm was left alone. He was the ruler of his world, and the feeling was enjoyable. The interview with Roberts took place because it was understood that GBS was the last court of appeal. Roberts, when sacked, had gone to the top man.

"Value for money," GBS said. "And from the reports on the table here I'm not getting it."

"I've been here more than twenty years."

"Twenty-two. What then?"

"Now I'm to be turned off with a month's notice."

"You feel you are being badly treated? Let us consider." There was nothing he enjoyed more than an argument of this kind, in which he held all the trump cards. "You came here and stayed here of your own free will. You worked as a packer and a machine hand, jobs that required no tradesman's skills, but still you were paid more than you would have been in a union shop. Your job, however, while involving no special skill, did demand that you should stand up at work. You tell me this is impossible—"

"It's my leg, my arthritis. You'd never believe the pain. The specialist, he says I must sit down, not all day, I got to keep moving, but just sit down sometimes, every half-hour. Standing's the worst thing for it, standing all day." Roberts was a small man with a drooping moustache. He spoke with the nasal whine of the area.

"Then of course you must sit down. But that means you are unable to do your job here."

"I'm being thrown on the scrapheap. No pension, nothing."

"You knew there was no pension scheme when you came—"

"I was young then, never thought about it."

"Please do not interrupt. You should have thought, you should have saved money. Now you must look for another job."

"With my leg, and me forty-seven years old, and unemployment

what it is, what chance have I got? You could find me another job
here, something behind a desk, easy enough if you wanted."

GBS never ceased to be polite, but now he allowed his
impatience to show. "Why should I do that? The reports I have
here don't suggest that you would be able to handle such work.
You have never worked behind a desk, you would be useless, and
we are not a charity. You must be logical, Mr Roberts. Value for
money is the rule between employer and employed. If you felt you
were worth more than we paid you, you were free to take another
job. Now you are no longer giving value for money. What more is
there to say?"

Roberts found other things to say, abusive and illogical things to
which GBS paid no attention. He would not have admitted even to
himself that he enjoyed such interviews, but he always found
pleasure in pointing out that the value for money argument was
irrefutable. The pleasure lasted during half of the forty-minute
drive home. Then he began to think about Paula.

He had married Paula ten years ago, when he was thirty-five and
she ten years younger. For some time he had felt no need to marry.
He had a flat in the heart of the city, and when it was necessary to
entertain for business purposes, a local firm sent in an excellent
cook, and a maid to serve the meal. Then he had interests, apart
from the firm, that kept him busy. He acknowledged the need to
keep fit, and like his namesake was a useful boxer. Games seemed
to him ridiculous, but he understood that they could be useful in
business terms, and made himself into an efficient golfer,
particularly on the greens, since putting seemed to him the most
logical part of the game. He went often to race meetings, where he
was a heavy punter. Was that illogical? Not so, for his bets were in
the service of the Emergency Fund. When he won he was paid in
cash, and the money went straight into a safe deposit account in
London. This was the Emergency Fund. It had been used on
several occasions when the use of cheques would have been
inadvisable.

He acknowledged also the need for sex. He took girls out,
sometimes for a day at the races, sometimes for dinner. Either way
they ended up in bed at the flat, a result he felt essential to justify
the time and money spent. A time came, however, when to his own

surprise he found all this unsatisfactory. He felt the need for a house of his own, for somebody to arrange those dinners, and to sit at one end of the table. A number of business acquaintances raised their eyebrows when they found that there was no hostess at his dinners, and he knew that there were always whispers about bachelors. Then again, a good deal of trouble in the sexual line would be saved if he had a wife. It would be a practical arrangement, she would be value for money. The right kind of wife, of course, somebody who looked on marriage as logically as he did himself.

He met Paula Mountford at a party, asked her to dinner and to the theatre, but made no attempt to take her to bed. He decided that she filled the bill perfectly. She was the younger daughter of a county family that had come down in the world, good-looking enough in a slightly awkward, big-boned way, and adept in keeping her conversational end up in any sort of company. She was also a girl with an eye on the main chance, something that was evident when he took her back to the flat, kissed her, and suggested that they should get married.

"You aren't in love with me."

"I don't talk about love, it's an abstraction. I find you attractive, and we seem to get on well."

"Well enough," she said coolly. She had a thick underlip, and it was stuck out now. "I don't love you, I'm not sure that I like you very much, but you're certain of yourself, you go out for what you want, and I admire that. At the moment you seem to want me. I suppose I should be flattered."

"I'm glad you're sensible."

"Not much use being anything else when you're around," she said with a laugh.

"I've got no time for romance, it seems to me nonsense. I think you should consider whether the advantages of being married to me are enough for you."

"All right. I'll tell you what I want. A wedding in style, church not registry office, no expense spared. A house outside the city, I hate bricks and mortar all round me. An acre or so of garden. My own car, a runabout. A couple of horses, I want to keep up my hunting. Good for your image to have a wife who hunts. A big dog, retriever or a labrador. A clothes account up in London, no complaints about how much I spend. That's all at the moment, though I shall think of other things I'm sure. In return I'll grace your table and share your bed. I don't suppose you want children?" He shook his head. "Luckily I'm not mad about them either."

"We agree about everything. It sounds as though you're good value for money." He smiled as he said it, but the words were serious.

"My God, you are a bastard." She pulled him to her. He was surprised, and disconcerted, by the ardency of her embrace.

Three months later Paula Mountford became Mrs George Bernard Shaw.

For years the arrangement had, it seemed to him, worked perfectly. Paula had everything she wanted. She had chosen the house, a large modern villa out in the country with a lot of ground, and outbuildings that were converted into a stable block. She had her horses, her golden retriever. She proved to be an excellent hostess, inventive with menus, skilful in making nervous guests feel at ease. She dressed individually and with flair, and he never said a word about bills. As for sex that rather lapsed, as he felt by mutual consent. He no longer felt much need for it, and the exercise of power in the firm was something that he found much more exciting. The firm prospered, his home life prospered. He was a contented man.

Until the day when he learned that Paula had a lover.

He learned it in the simplest way. He had mislaid his cigarette lighter, looked in an old bag of hers in the hope of finding one, and there was the letter. He was an incurious man, and would not have read it except that the word 'Darling' caught his eye. The words on the page seemed to him hardly credible. Could it be Paula to whom these phrases were addressed, embarrassing and ridiculous phrases of a kind that he would never have been able to bring himself to put down on paper? Paula was up in London, and it was typical of him that his first action after making the discovery was to go on looking for a light, and then to smoke his cigarette before reading the letter again.

He congratulated himself on this calmness, but it was succeeded by a wave of anger such as he had never known. The anger had no outward manifestation, he did not break any of Paula's things or cut up her clothes, but the emotion shook him as he had not been shaken since he was eleven years old. He had been told then by his father that his mother had left the house forever, and gone to live with another man. He had felt that as a personal betrayal, a possession he had lost, and now he felt the same thing. Paula belonged to him, he had given her everything she ever asked for, and she had now deliberately betrayed him. She must be punished.

He made a copy of the letter, and returned it to the bag. It was, again, typical of him that he did not consider asking the name of her lover, or whether the affair was over. Such questions might lead to argument, and he only argued from a position of assured superiority. Should he employ a private detective? He decided against this, partly because it was Paula's betrayal that concerned him and not the name of her past or present lover, but principally for the reason that to consult a private detective involved putting himself to some extent in the man's power, and to put himself in somebody else's power was something that he had never done in his life. Instead he watched Paula himself, following her by car on the days when she said that she would be going out. He did not use his own car, which she might have recognized, but rented one. In less than a week he had discovered the identity of her lover. He was a man of Paula's own age, divorced from his wife, a well-to-do gentleman farmer who was a member of the hunt she rode with. The man lived a few miles away, and she went to his house one or two afternoons a week.

But GBS was little interested in the man, and did not blame him. He appreciated that to sleep with another man's wife was a kind of triumph, one he had savoured himself in his bachelor days, when the chief pleasure had been talking afterwards to the unwitting cuckold. It was Paula who must be punished, but it was easier to say this than to discover the means. He did not threaten divorce, because he feared that this would be no punishment, and also it would mean that she was no longer in his possession. What else could he do that would make her miserable as she deserved to be miserable, take away forever that look of a cat almost choked with cream that he now saw on her face? He thought about it for days while the anger grew within him, grew satisfyingly because he knew that it would find an outlet. Eventually he decided that the only possible punishment was death.

It was necessary to assure himself that the punishment was just, and this was not difficult. Look at the matter logically, and it was apparent that he and Paula had an agreement. She had broken it, and no longer gave value for the money she received. It was true, and he acknowledged it, that the idea of her suffering pleased him, as he had been pleased by the lasting nature of the injuries sustained by that trade union branch secretary. He considered, and reluctantly rejected, the idea that Paula's horse face might be permanently scarred. What would happen afterwards? He could hardly divorce her without incurring blame, and he had no wish to spend the rest of his life with a disfigured woman.

He was aware that the logic he used was that of a superior man (in a phrase, the logic of GBS), and that it would not be generally understood. In the event of Paula's death he would be an obvious suspect, and he had no intention of standing in a dock, or even suffering arrest. It was essential therefore that he should not have any apparent connection with what happened. He would work through intermediaries, but none of them must see him, or be able to make a connection leading back to him. It was a difficult problem, but one of an intellectual kind, resembling a problem in chess. He played chess well, and in a day or two he had solved the problem.

The first person to see was Jerry Wilde. Jerry owed him a debt, but he would not rely on that. The logical man does not depend on emotion.

The debts Jerry owed him, for they were counted in the plural, went back to their days at grammar school. GBS had always been, like his namesake, long and wiry, physically capable of looking after himself. Jerry Wilde was the kind of perky little shrimp who was a natural target for bullying. It had been amusing to defend him, and to show his contempt for the rest of the school by making it clear that he would sooner talk to Jerry than to the captain of cricket. Jerry's worshipful attitude, his readiness to run errands and in general to do what he was told, were also agreeable. He was a lively little boy, an excellent mimic, good especially at catching

the tones of other boys, and a great success in the school plays. But
there was a basic dishonesty about Jerry. He would cheat in exams
even though he knew the answers, and GBS had once saved him
from the threat of expulsion for stealing, by pretending to find the
missing money, which he had provided out of his own pocket.

Jerry's later career was much what might have been predicted.
He got jobs but couldn't hold them. He went on benders and failed
to turn up for work, fiddled accounts when he had anything to do
with money, was always ready to help in handling TV sets, cases of
whisky, or other quickly saleable things without asking where they
came from. GBS had saved him from an embezzlement charge by
paying his employer something over the amount Jerry had taken,
and from something more serious when Jerry, blind drunk at the
wheel of a car, had mounted the pavement and knocked down an
old age pensioner. She had been persuaded to take money instead
of pressing charges. Why did he bother with Jerry? Well, on both
those occasions he had made Jerry sign a statement admitting the
facts. And then Jerry seemed to know or be able to get the dirt on
everybody, and GBS had made use of his knowledge. It was Jerry
who had found the boys who turned the trick with the vans and
those who tamed the trade unionists, who told them what to do
and paid them off, so that GBS never even knew who they were.
Jerry was useful.

At the moment he was working for a man who cannibalized
cars, put bits and pieces into other cars that had been in accidents
and sold for scrap. Then he sprayed them, changed the speedo and
plates, and sold them as salesman's models.

"Looking for a car, boss? Give you a good trade-in on the one
you've got." Jerry had always been a grinner. Above the grin his
nose was bright red with alcohol, his cheeks hardly less so.

"I wanted a chat."

"Round at the King's Head?" GBS shook his head, made a
gesture towards his car. "Like that, is it? Mind the shop, Bill, shan't
be long." Bill, at the back of the showroom, waved a hand. They
drove a couple of miles, then GBS pulled into a lay-by.

"You're going to land in trouble with those cars," he said. "The
registration plate on that Jaguar, where did it come from?"

"Couldn't tell you offhand."

"And what about the registration book?"

"Looks beautiful. Don't ask where I got it, not unless you're a buyer."

"You won't get away with it for long."

"And when there's trouble who shall I run to? Don't tell me. Did we come out here for you to say that, or just to look at the traffic?"

"Neither. I need a little help."

Jerry cocked his head to one side, bird-like. "Yours to command."

"It's a little bit like the Layton business." Layton had sustained the hip injury.

"And you want me to find a couple of boys, fix it with them?"

"Not exactly. I want somebody reliable, very reliable. You find him, give me a number where I can call him. You don't, not on any account, mention my name. That's it."

"That's it?" Jerry's bright bird-eye showed surprise. "You'll handle it yourself? Why and wherefore?"

"Not your business. You just give me a name and number."

"The boss orders, it shall be done." He sketched a salute. "A bit ticklish though. The sort of boy I know, he knows me. But he *don't* know you, if you get my meaning. If I knew the strength of what you wanted, that would help."

"No. It's better to stick to what I said."

"That means it must be strong."

He affected irritation. "If you don't want to help, say so. There'd be fifty pounds in it for you, just for a name and number."

"When have I ever said no? It's ticklish, that's all. I might have to put you on to somebody who'd pass you on, get me? Leave it with me for a day or two, I'll ask around. Discreetly mind, don't worry. That's it?"

"That's it."

"Then let's get back." When they were back at the showroom Jerry stuck his head through the car window. His breath smelt of beer and pickled onions. "About the fifty, GBS, forget it. This one's on the house."

Two days later he rang back with a name and number. "Like I said, it's someone who'll make the arrangements. Can't say more, he'll tell you the rest himself. Say you're a friend of mine when you call. Ring at five o'clock any afternoon, he'll be there. And, boss?"

"Yes?"

"Be careful. They're wide awake, some of these boys."

The thought of the dangerous element involved made his blood tingle, his heart beat pleasurably faster. The danger of involvement was part of the game, its avoidance a mark of the logician's skill. Had Jerry understood that? In any case his part was now finished, and he could say nothing damaging.

He rang the number from a public call-box just after five o'clock. The voice that came on was low, cautious.

"Is that Mr Middleton, Jack Middleton?"

"Yes."

"Jerry Wilde gave me your name, said I could call you."

"Jerry, right."

"He thought you might be able to help me with a problem."

"What sort of problem?"

"A friend of mine needs a job done."

Now the voice rose a little, roughened, a voice definitely not out of the top drawer.

"I don't know that you're talking about. Who are you, what's your name?"

"My friend wants me to remain private."

"Is that so? You just tell him my name's Jack Middleton and I like to know who I'm dealing with. Got it?"

"Yes. Don't hang up, Mr Middleton. We're talking about a big job, a lot of money."

Silence. "How much is a lot? And what's it for?"

"My friend wants—" He found, quite unexpectedly, that he could not form the words. He was strongly conscious of the interior of the telephone-box. On one wall somebody had written *Tony loves Lucy* and on another *United Rule OK?*.

The harsh voice said, "What's up? Wants somebody hit, is that it?"

Hit, did that mean killed? He was not sure. "Disposed of." The words came out choked, as if he was being strangled.

"Say it how you like. Ten grand."

"How much?"

"Ten grand. That covers it, my commission included."

He was so astonished that he was briefly silent. He wanted to expostulate, to say that the jobs done before had cost no more than a few hundred, but very likely Middleton knew nothing about them. When he found his voice he said, "That's much more than my friend expected. It's too much."

"Please yourself. That's the price."

"I must—must consult. I take it nothing would be payable until—"

"Half in advance, other half when it's done."

"But that would be trusting you with five thousand pounds."

"Who's trusting who, mister?" the coarse voice asked. "I don't even know your bloody name."

He left the box a little shaken. He was so used to being in a position of mastery, to dealing with everybody as he had dealt with Roberts, that to be almost in the position of a supplicant was disconcerting. Perhaps he should give up the whole thing, tell Paula that he knew of her affair and threaten to cut off her allowance and stop her charge accounts? But supposing she ignored him, supposing she went off to live with her gentleman farmer and made him a laughing-stock? Even the possibility was not to be contemplated.

That weekend they gave a dinner party. The food was delicious, Paula as usual an admirable hostess, but he felt half a dozen times during the evening that she was mocking him. When the guests had gone he felt such a wave of fury that he could have strangled her, or shot her with the old Webley that he had inherited from his father, who had fancied himself as a shot and had set up a target in the back garden. In fact the revolver was in his desk drawer and they were talking in the bedroom, so that the question of such a spontaneous action did not arise. In any event it would of course have been stupid, illogical, unworthy of GBS. But that evening made him decide to go ahead. On Monday evening he rang Middleton again, calling as he had been told to do at five o'clock.

"I've talked to my friend. He'd like to go ahead. On the lines you mentioned."

"What's his name? Your *friend*, I mean."

"No names. That's a condition."

"All right." There was an unexpected chuckle. "But there's one name you gotta give me, what you might call the subject." GBS gave Paula's name, and their address. "You never said it was a woman."

He replied with a touch of his usual acerbity. "Before we were just talking. Now it's serious, and there are things I want to know. Is your agent reliable? Does it make any difference to him that it's a woman?"

"Makes no odds to him, it's just a job. He was one of those what you call 'em, mercenaries, out in Angola, freelance now. You can talk to him yourself, make up your own mind."

"I don't want to meet him."

"You don't have to. I said talk, not meet. I'll give you a number to ring, ask for Charlie."

"About making payment—"

"Talk to Charlie. You fix it with him, you pay him, he gives me my cut. He knows there might be a job, so just mention me. Here's the number." He gave it. "Just one thing, he ain't always there. I'd call in the evening, between six and eight. After eight he's usually out with the boys."

"He's reliable, he wouldn't talk about it to them?"

"He's a professional."

The first time he rang the number there was no reply. The second time a voice answered, and said it was Charlie.

"I've been put on to you by Jack Middleton. About a job I want done."

"Jack said something, gave me the name. And you're Mr X, incognito you might call it." The voice had a disagreeable twang to it, some accent he could not place. Was it South African? Charlie began asking practical questions. When did he want it done? As soon as possible. GBS had given some thought to the method, and said that if it could look like a car accident, that would be ideal. Charlie said a decisive no to that, as too hard to arrange. Then an attempted burglary of the house, the subject came home unexpectedly—

The voice with its odd twang interrupted. "You've been reading too many books, Mr X. First thing I look after is Number One. It's got to be simple, probably at night, a gun with a silencer. If I can make it look like a robbery okay, but don't rely on it. Don't rely on anything, except the job being done."

"When?"

"Give me a week after I've got the first instalment. Let's talk about that. I want used notes, ones and fives. You drop it by a rubbish bin on the London road, I pick it up, I'll give you the details."

"No."

For the first time the voice lost its assurance. "What you mean, no?"

"That won't do. You could check on my car or see me. You said I'm incognito. I want to stay that way. Now, this is what I propose."

Charlie listened, then said, "And the other five? When the job's done?"

"The same way."

"Fancy but clever. Think of everything, Mr X, don't you?"

"I try to." Then they discussed the timing.

The conversation took place on Monday evening. On Wednesday afternoon GBS took the two-thirty train out of the city. It was a slow train that stopped at several places, and it was busy during the rush hours but two-thirds empty in the afternoons, so that he had no trouble in finding a carriage to himself.

When he was a boy they had lived at Thelsby, almost at the end of the line, and he had travelled hundreds of times on the train to school. A couple of miles before Thelsby there was a stretch of single-track line, and the train from the city always stopped to let one from the other direction come through. At the point where it stopped there was a grass embankment to one side, and often in that distant past he and Jerry had jumped out of the carriage, half-run and half-rolled down the grass, leapt down the steep bank at the end, and wriggled through the wire that separated the embankment from the road.

Today the train stopped as it had always done. GBS muffled his face in a scarf. There was a whistle, the train for the city passed them. He opened the carriage window. Their own train began to move, very slowly. He flung the cheap attaché case as far as he could down the grass slope. He could see no sign of Charlie, who was no doubt concealed behind the steep drop at the bottom. All Charlie could have seen of him was a hand, and a face hidden behind a scarf. On the way back from Thelsby he looked out to where he had thrown the attaché case, and saw only grass.

It was perfect.

He recited the perfection of it to himself all the way home. It was inevitable that after Paula's death all three people involved, Jerry, Jack and Charlie, should assume that he had ordered it. Let them think so, for they could prove nothing. And what could the police prove? If they talked to Jerry, any admission he made would be damaging to himself, and so could be ruled out. As for Jack Middleton and Charlie, what identification could they make beyond a voice on the telephone?

Of course he would be a suspect. He was prepared for long interrogations, and even looked forward to them because he knew that he would emerge triumphant. No doubt the police would discover the gentleman farmer, but this revelation would come as a total surprise to GBS. (How wise he had been not to use a private detective.) And the police would look in vain for any discrepancies in his bank account, or any large withdrawals, for the money had come from the Emergency Fund. Would he pay the rest of the money after the job was done? He kept an open mind about it, feeling that it must be possible to make some deal with Charlie.

It was a logical operation, and in such an operation every possibility is taken into account, so that the unexpected cannot occur. He had only to sit back and await the result.

Thursday passed, and Friday. He drove into the works as usual, chaired editorial discussions, had talks with a consortium that was talking about making an offer for two of his weeklies. While he went about these occupations he waited for the telephone call, or for the policeman who would begin: "I'm sorry to say, Mr Shaw, that . . ." On Friday afternoon, he knew, Paula saw her farmer. Perhaps while she was driving home . . . or when she returned to the house . . . ?

But when he returned on Friday he was greeted by the smell of boeuf bourguignon and found Paula in the kitchen, making a first course of avocado and prawns. She had the *sleek* look she always wore after a session with her lover, a look that dissipated any possible feeling of regret. On Saturday Paula went out with the hunt, on Sunday morning the papers were late and she drove down to the village to get them. Each time he wound himself up into a state of expectation, but nothing happened. On Sunday evening he was unable to sit still to watch TV, made an excuse and went to his study, where he sat at his desk staring out into the dark night. When he returned she was watching a gangster series.

On Monday morning she said that she was going to London. Whether she did so, or saw her farmer, she was at home in the evening.

On Tuesday nothing happened.

Give me a week after I've got the first instalment. On Wednesday afternoon the week was up. And on that evening Paula came home in the best of spirits after, as she said, an afternoon spent with a couple of girl friends. They were giving a dinner party on Friday, and she had done some shopping for it.

On Thursday morning he left home as usual, went to a call-box and rang Charlie's number. No reply. He drove in to the works, dealt with correspondence, went out twice to call-boxes. The number rang, but there was no answer. Ring between six and eight in the evening, Jack Middleton had said. He rang at six with no result, and then called the exchange to ask if the line was in working order. In less than a minute the operator came back to him.

"That number is a public call-box."

"*What?* It isn't possible. There must be a mistake."

"I will repeat the number," the operator said, and did so. "Is that correct? Very good. That is the number of a public call-box."

He asked where it was, and was given the name of a street in the east end of the city. He drove down there, looked at the red glass-windowed box, even went into it as though there might be an answer to his questions within. In some way or other he had been cheated, either by Charlie or by Jack Middleton. He did not ring Middleton, but went to see Jerry Wilde.

Jerry was in the King's Head, drinking what was obviously not his first or second brandy and soda. He greeted GBS with a slap on the back, and asked how things were going.

"I have to talk to you. Come out now. Right away."

"Can't be done, boss. Got to meet a man about a car. Big deal.

Be here any minute. Then taking him out for a drive, back here, have a couple of drinks, argue the toss about the price—"

It might just have been possible to talk sense to Jerry now, but in an hour or two it would be useless to try.

"Come and see me tomorrow."

"Anything you say. When and where?"

On Friday there was a meeting at the office which was likely to take all day. He told Jerry to come to the house at six o'clock. He would be long gone before seven-thirty, when the dinner-party guests arrived.

"Unexpected honour, boss. I'll be there." It was true that Jerry was not the kind of person he asked home, and that Paula did not care for him, but the circumstances were exceptional.

On Friday, punctually at six, Jerry drove up in a Jaguar, no doubt the one with the fake registration book. He wore a hat with a little feather in it, and a check suit. Paula was passing through the hall on the way to the kitchen when he arrived, and greeted him coolly. After that they went to the study. GBS sat behind his desk and told Jerry what had happened. At the end he said, "I want an explanation."

Jerry wriggled. "You know what you sound like? Old Porson, our old head. *I want an explanation, Wilde.* And I knew I'd never be able to explain, not to his satisfaction. You wouldn't have a drink handy?"

"After the explanation."

"I only put you in touch with Jack Middleton. Have you tried ringing him?"

"No. It was Charlie who arranged to take the money."

"Trouble is I don't know Charlie, do I? Why not try Jack, see what he's got to say? Here, I'll dial the number for you, I know it." He did so, and held up the receiver so that GBS could hear the ringing tone. Then he dialled again.

"What are you doing?"

"Just checking. Operator, will you run a check on one-eight-three-four-six. I've been dialling, and can't get a reply. What's that, what do you say? Well I never. Many thanks." He put down the telephone, grinned. "Would you believe it, that's a public call-box."

"But that isn't possible. You put me in touch with Middleton."

"That's right."

"You must know him."

"Right again, boss, I know him." Out of Jerry Wilde's grinning face came the rough voice. *"You just tell him my name's Jack Middleton.* I know Charlie too." And GBS heard again that disagreeable twang. *"You've been reading too many stories, Mr X. The first thing I look after is Number One.* I was always able to manage voices, remember?"

Even now he could not believe it. "The attaché case. It was you who collected it."

"Nobody else. I thought it was a nice touch, dropping it where we used to scramble down as kids. Sentimental. Nearly piped my eye."

"You've robbed me, stolen five thousand pounds."

Jerry's grin became a laugh. "I don't see it that way. I reckon you owe it me."

"But I've always helped you. I kept you out of prison."

"And made me sign statements so that you could hold 'em over me. Only you can't use 'em now, can you, or you'd have to say why you hung on to them so long. Did you think I liked being an errand boy? Anyway, the answer's no. So when you were so mysterious I thought, well, let's see just what he's got in mind, shall we. And my word, wasn't it naughty?" Jerry wiped his red face with a handkerchief and went on.

"I wouldn't try again to do something naughty about your wife, because I might have something interesting to tell the fuzz. And you can't do anything about the five thousand, can you, *boss?* I'm taking a holiday for a few weeks, can't make up my mind whether it's Madeira or the West Indies, but before I went I wanted to see your face when I told you. Incidentally, I bet you meant to cheat poor old Charlie out of his second five grand. Do you know where I'd say you are, boss? Up the creek without a paddle."

Before this speech was half-way through, George Bernard Shaw had ceased to be a logical and reasonable man, and had become a machine filled with nothing but hatred for the creature opposite him. He acted not reasonably, but from this uncontrollable hatred when he opened the right-hand drawer of the desk, took out the revolver, and shot Jerry Wilde neatly between the eyes.

George Bernard Shaw went to Broadmoor. There he became the chess champion, and every month composed a chess problem which he sent to the world champion, challenging him to solve it. From the fact that he never received any reply to these communications he made the logical deduction that the champion was unable to solve the problems, and by the extension of this logic that George Bernard Shaw was the best chess player in the world.

HOUSE POISON

Antonia Fraser

I CAN DATE the beginning of the whole melancholy business quite
clearly. It was that bet, I said. That's what I told the detective,
Tomlinson. After all I was in a privileged position, wasn't I? I saw
it all.

"We both were," said Bella, adding in that reproving little voice
of hers: "We both looked after the Colonel and Lady Sissy." Then
she clicks her tongue, a thoroughly maddening habit.

To return to the beginning: the bet. Let's face it, Bella was in the
kitchen and *I* was getting them their drinks, their PPs, as the
Colonel always called them. PP for pre-prandial. He had
nicknames for everything, everything to do with drink that is.
Posties were post-prandial drinks (not many of those allowed) and
MMs, mid-morning drinks, were even rarer: heavy colds or
birthdays were about the only things which justified an MM in my
experience.

As I told that fellow Tomlinson, the Colonel was never a heavy
drinker in all the years I was at the Manor and believe me I know
what I'm talking about. But he was an *opinionated* drinker. I had to
explain this several times to Tomlinson before he got the point and
then he said something typical like: "He could afford to have
opinions, I suppose," looking around at the Manor in that
offensive way of his.

"Manor or no Manor, he was an opinionated man in every
way," I countered, and hoping to tease: "Opinionated *gentleman*, I
should say." But Tomlinson just sighed, so I ended: "Naturally he
had opinions about drinks."

And that was really how it all began. Drink. The papers called it
POISON AT THE MANOR HOUSE and all that kind of rubbish, but it
wasn't anything to do with the Manor, leastways not how they

meant it, it was to do with whisky, whisky versus cocktails. The Colonel's "medicinal whisky" in his own phrase versus Lady Sissy's "house poison" as she used to call her famous cocktail.

"House poison for me, Henry," she would say in that high fluting voice of hers. I can hear it in my ears now; odd how it carried without being half as strong as the Colonel's voice, carried right through the Manor.

"Henry!" rising on the last syllable. "Henry!" Sometimes in the kitchen Bella would put her hands over her ears.

"She's not calling *me*," she would say, as if the tone of voice was somehow my fault.

At this point I would mix Lady Sissy's special cocktail, at least on the good days I mixed it, because I'm sure I never put in half the vodka she did when she mixed it, vodka and whatever else; whereas I, I laid on the grapefruit juice pretty strong (that's what made it the *house* poison—the grapefruit juice—as Lady Sissy explained to me when I first arrived).

"Whenever I say 'house poison', Henry, that's what I want."

"Why don't you just ask for poison straight up?" the Colonel grunted. As he did, in almost exactly the same words, on so many other occasions. That was the point: the Colonel and Lady Sissy swore by their own particular tipple—no harm in that since they were rich enough to afford it, as someone like Tomlinson would be sure to point out. The trouble was that they could never leave it at that: always on at each other on the subject. All a struggle for domination, says I, having studied psychology by post a year or two back: Bella didn't approve, but I pointed out that it would help me deal with the old couple (and save me going mad with the monotony, I might have added, but didn't, Bella being obviously part of the monotony).

The only wonder was that the Colonel and Lady Sissy had been living together all these years. But then:

"No choice, have they?" says Bella; for I have to admit that it's Bella, sharp-eyes Bella who has discovered about the contents of the will. At which point I should explain that the Colonel— Colonel the Honourable Lionel Blake, to give him his full name—and Lady Sissy—the Lady Agnes Cecilia Mary Blake, to give her hers—were brother and sister. And the will in question was their father's, the old Earl of Blakesmoor. The family estate went to the eldest son of course, and had passed in turn to *his* son, the twelfth Earl, a dreadful young man who asked us to call him Blakey. We didn't enjoy his visits, I can tell you.

"Bohemian is the word for him," says Bella on one occasion, finding him with a garlic crusher in her kitchen. (I thought I spotted an Oedipus complex there.)

To return to our couple: in his will, the old Earl had been able to separate the Manor from the family estate because it had been part of his wife's dowry. Neither the Colonel nor Lady Sissy had ever married, so the old Earl left them the Manor property jointly: on condition they lived in it together. And looked after each other. He used those very words in his will, Bella told me. If either of them left the house, the other one inherited the whole property.

So there they were, stuck with it. Although many might say that we did the looking after. But then they were both well over seventy at the time we answered the advertisement. Did I mention that by the old Earl's will, the Manor finally got left to the survivor? Provided the Colonel and Lady Sissy had remained together, that is. Because that was the situation. And that's what lay underneath it all, in my opinion, that was the power struggle beneath the quarrelling about the drinks. Who was going to be the survivor? With the Colonel swearing that whisky made you live forever because it was so healthy and Lady Sissy declaring in her high-pitched voice: "Live forever, Lionel? How can you be so absurd? Whisky or no whisky, I shall outlive you, see if I don't." At which she would call for another "house poison" and drink it with the kind of dainty relish you could see was intended to drive the Colonel mad.

All the same, for all the rows, they did manage to stick together. And they lived to a ripe old age, what's more. Which says something for both the Colonel's medicinal whisky *and* Lady Sissy's house poison. I made Lady Sissy eighty at least when the tragedy happened and the Colonel was only a couple of years younger. Drink had certainly not cut short *their* lives. Because the Colonel was as hale and hearty an old gentleman as you could hope to find and even Lady Sissy kept on gardening right to the end. Well, they both gardened as a matter of fact, that was another thing they kept arguing about. Lady Sissy only got a bit tottery at that time of day when the cocktails had got to her, or to put it another way, she to the cocktails. The Colonel never tottered.

If only they hadn't been quite so vigorous! So determined, both of them, to survive the other. A bit more tottering or doddering about the place and they might have been content to let nature take its course, lean on each other a bit, be glad not to be living alone like so many old people must. As it was, there was so much vigour about, that the arguments if anything got worse. Especially at PP time. Which brings me to the evening of the bet.

"Lionel!" I heard her fluting away, as I stood at the drinks tray, shaking away at the silver cocktail mixer. "You've been wrong about everything for over seventy-five years! Why not admit you're wrong now?"

"Prove it, Sissy," the Colonel grunted. "Just prove it." Up till then, to be honest, I hadn't been listening very carefully; thought it was the same mixture as before, as in my silver shaker.

"I *will* prove it," exclaimed Lady Sissy in a voice which was suddenly a good deal stronger, a good deal less fluttery than the voice she generally used; something of the old Earl's military bearing (there's a big portrait of him over the fireplace) had evidently got into her. Then: "Henry! Take away the Colonel's glass. No, no, you silly man. Don't fill it up."

I suppose I just stood there, staring at her. Nothing in my psychological studies had prepared me for this one, I can tell you.

And: "Give me the bottle, Henry," she went on. "We'll have it locked up. No, on second thoughts, *you* lock it up, Henry, and give me the key. There's going to be no cheating, Lionel, you've been cheating as well for over seventy-five years. The whisky will be locked up for a month. You're perfectly healthy now: we just had Dr Salmon over and he said so. We'll have him over again at the end of the month and he'll tell us honestly whether there's any difference. I assure you, Lionel, there won't be any difference, none at all. Then we'll know what sort of value to put on your famous medicinal whisky.

"It's a bet," she ended. "We'll write it in the betting book." This was a heavy red leather number, quite antique, with the Blakesmoor arms on it. It had once belonged to the old Earl; some of the ancient bets in it had to be read to be believed, what those officers got up to! As Bella remarked, when she was dusting it: "They didn't deserve to *have* horses, did they?"

But the Colonel and Lady Sissy had been using it for years, writing down their own bets. When I had to show it to Tomlinson, I couldn't help hoping he wouldn't go to the front of the book, the old bets being such grist to his mill, to put it mildly. But of course he did. Speechless for a while and then coming out with something predictable like: "So this is our aristocracy. Roll on the revolution."

The Colonel's bets were really quite tame stuff compared to what had gone before, Lady Sissy's too: although there were an awful lot of them. It was typical of Tomlinson that he was out to sneer at the feebleness of the old couple's bets, just after being so fearfully shocked by their father's scandalous ones.

"What a lot of fuss about—" He stopped. Well, he couldn't quite say it was a fuss about nothing, could he? In view of what had occurred. Myself, I had always looked at that red leather book as an important symbol in the power struggle even if I was a little slow to appreciate the serious nature of this particular bet, out of all the others.

"What exactly is the bet, m'lady?" I asked politely as I carried the big book over to her. I sometimes wrote the bets down for them, and they signed them; although on this occasion it was Lady Sissy herself who wrote it down—frankly, I don't think I would have dared write it, not with the Colonel there glowering at me.

"The bet is that the Colonel will drink no whisky for a month, at the end of which he will be passed fit as a fiddle by Dr Salmon. That's the bet. Agreed, Lionel?"

I looked at the Colonel. His face had gone quite red and for a moment I thought—but no, he recovered himself. He continued to sit there staring at Lady Sissy as if he couldn't quite believe his own ears.

"You're trying to kill me," he said at length. He spoke quite slowly as if he had just discovered something of major importance about his sister after all these years. "You're trying to kill me by robbing me of my whisky. Prove it, indeed. That'll prove nothing. Because I shall be dead, shan't I? I'll be proved right that the whisky was keeping me alive; but then it'll be too late. I'll be in my grave and you'll be alive and here at the Manor—"

"Stuff and nonsense, Lionel," replied Lady Sissy airily, as she sipped away at her own cocktail. "Since I don't believe in all this medicinal business anyway, it's my opinion that far from being in your grave you'll be in even better health at the end of the month than before! And that's what Dr Salmon will tell us."

The Colonel continued to gaze at her.

"So what about PPs?" he asked after a while in a gruff voice. "What do I drink then? Cocoa?" By Jove, I thought, he's going to do it. He's going to take the bet. And sure enough he pulled the big red leather book towards him and signed the bet which Lady Sissy had written, with a flourish. No question about the signature there, as even Tomlinson had to agree, he entered into it of his own free will.

"You could drink some of my house—" began Lady Sissy and then thought better of it at the sight of the Colonel's beetling brows; also his face had begun to go red again.

"Some sherry, sir?" I suggested brightly.

"I shall drink nothing," pronounced the Colonel in a sonorous tone, ignoring me. "If I can't drink whisky, I shan't drink anything. I shall sit here for a month at PPs and watch you, Sissy, drink yourself to death with that disgusting mixture of yours. At the end of the month, when my constitution will have become greatly weakened, and I shall therefore have won the bet, you will pay me by giving up drinking that rubbish."

"What?" Lady Sissy almost choked on her glass. "No more house poison if you win? You're being ridiculous."

"That's the bet," said the Colonel implacably. He wrote it in the book. "Sign it, Sissy."

"What does it matter since I'm going to win?" Lady Sissy sounded quite petulant as she spoke; nevertheless she signed the book in her turn.

"You'll be grateful to me, Sissy. That rubbish is going to be the death of you one day—"

"Stuff and nonsense, Lionel," cried Lady Sissy, good humour restored as she lifted the glass which I had refilled. "Stuff and nonsense." It was her favourite expression where the Colonel was concerned. Whatever he suggested, Lady Sissy was inclined to come back at him with that phrase: "Stuff and nonsense, you're talking nonsense as usual, Lionel," she would exclaim, fluting away.

Unfortunately for once the Colonel wasn't talking stuff and nonsense. Three weeks later, it *was* the house poison which killed her. Or rather, to be precise, it was the poison—weedkiller, paraquat—which was contained in the house poison which killed her. Ironically enough weedkillers generally were one of the topics the Colonel and Lady Sissy were always arguing about. Always on at each other about the state of the garden shed, too, and who had the key last, that sort of thing. As I told Tomlinson, who was scarcely surprised, they used to argue about anything. And everything.

Weedkiller: a horrible death. I'm glad I wasn't present when it actually took place. The Colonel mixed that last cocktail for her himself, waiting till I was out of the room. That's what the police think must have happened. Thank God I didn't see it: it was bad enough seeing her body afterwards. Poor old girl.

But I was present when he died too, very shortly afterwards. Poor old boy. That was enough horror for me, I can tell you. He asked me for the key, looking absolutely crazy, a mad glint in his eye, his face quite red; he was breathing so heavily that I thought he was going to have a stroke. That was before I knew what he had done, of course. It seemed more natural afterwards, as I told Tomlinson, that he should be in such a state.

At the time he just asked me for the key of the whisky cupboard: "Time for my PP, Henry," was what he said, not mentioning Lady Sissy at all. It wasn't my place to question him, not my place to ask where she was, let alone my place to point out that the month wasn't quite up . . . I just gave it to him and saw him lope off in the direction of the cellar, with that curious strong stride he had, right till the very last moment, a healthy vigorous man. Till he drank the whisky, that is. I can still hear his cry now, ringing in my ears. I came running. Bella came running (it takes a lot to move Bella out of her kitchen but the noise of the Colonel's death throes got even Bella moving).

It was too late. You can try of course, and as I told Tomlinson, we tried, all the well-known remedies, milk, bicarb, we tried everything. But it was much too late. She had absolutely laced that bottle with the stuff, knowing how he'd fall upon it once the month of the bet was over. The police told me afterwards—not Tomlinson, another man, more practical, not so full of social theories—that she'd given him a far, far bigger dose than he gave her. But then they say that, don't they? About the female of the species being deadlier than the male.

She must have planned it well in advance: they found her fingerprints all over the bottle. She must have sat there waiting for the time to be up, and knowing that the famous medicinal whisky was going to kill him. As for him, it seems that his was more of a spontaneous gesture, the weedkiller put into the cocktail shaker at the last moment, finding the sight of her drinking away at their regular PPs quite intolerable. And spiking it with the weedkiller. Mad really. Never knowing that by that time she'd done for him too. Mad really, the pair of them. Poor old boy, poor old girl: there was something childish about them, to tell you the truth, childish as well as crazy. Perhaps that's what comes of living with your brother and sister all your life. Psychologically retarded.

"Not quite natural, was it?" said Bella afterwards, clicking her tongue. "When you think of what it says in the Bible about man cleaving to his wife."

But Tomlinson put it another way: "A class tragedy", was how he saw it. In short, property had ruined their lives. Without the Manor or the hope of the Manor, they would have been just another nice old couple living in retirement. We had to tell the police all about the quarrels, naturally, and of course the fatal bet which finally turned the Colonel's brain. Then the lawyers told the police about the will, and how everything was due to go to the survivor: that must have preyed on Lady Sissy and in the end driven her mad too.

"Property is theft," pronounced Tomlinson solemnly, with the air of one who has found the right quotation.

Property is theft indeed. I had to hide my smile. As a detective, he really would have done far better to study psychology like me, instead of all this sociological nonsense. As I said to Bella long afterwards, when we were clearing up the Manor for the young

Earl—who inherited it back again—we shan't need to go thieving in the future, now we've got enough for our own little property. A very substantial legacy indeed on condition we stayed to the end of their lives; and nobody can say we didn't do that. It was once again sharp-eyes Bella who found out all about our legacy.

But it's no good Bella claiming credit for everything. The weedkiller was entirely my idea. Not that I handled a drop of it myself: far too dangerous. Besides, where was the need to handle the poison personally when I had all the resources of psychology at my command? The way I handled that old couple, once the fatal bet was struck, made me rather fancy myself as a kind of latter-day Iago. I tried that one on Bella but she only sniffed. It's possible of course that Bella doesn't know who Iago is, since Bella, for all her sharpness, had never really bothered to improve her mind. I sometimes wonder—

"All the same, Henry, we're a good team," said Bella suddenly, just as I was thinking about her lack of culture. Bella can be quite a mind-reader at times, even if she lacks culture. "That detective, Tomlinson, told me that it did him good to come across a proper working marriage like ours, a proper partnership. So we have to stick together, don't we? Just like the Colonel and Lady Sissy. We don't want to disappoint Tomlinson."

And Bella began sipping her pre-prandial drink—it was a sherry, as a matter of fact, a newly acquired habit with our new prosperity—with a delicate gesture that reminded me of Lady Sissy. If only Bella didn't make little sucking noises! (Lady Sissy never made any noise at all when she drank.) Ah well—

"House poison," says I, pouring myself some of the Colonel's whisky.

A SENSE OF HISTORY

Michael Gilbert

"YOU ARE MY Member," said Colonel Mounteagle.

"Indeed, yes," said Mr Pocock, sipping nervously at the glass of sherry which the colonel had thrust on to him when he arrived.

"You represent my interests in Parliament."

"Yours, and other people's."

"Never mind about other people. It isn't other people's land this feeder road is going to ruin. It's my land."

"That's one way of looking at it," agreed Mr Pocock. "But you have to bear in mind that by taking the pressure off the road between your lodge gates and the roundabout, a number of people with houses on that stretch will be relieved of the heavy flow of traffic just outside their front gates. Danger to children—"

"Irrelevant," said the colonel. "People who buy houses on the main road must expect to see a bit of traffic. That's not the point. When a road is going to invade the privacy of a landowner—is going to trespass across *his* fields—he *must* be allowed some say in the matter. That's right, isn't it?"

"Up to a point."

"Right. Have some more sherry." Without allowing Mr Pocock to say yes or no he refilled his glass. "Now, you've got a chance to do what's needed. You've drawn a place—third place, I believe—in the ballot for private members' bills. I've told you what's wanted. A simple three- or four-clause bill saying that where a new road is planned the landowners affected by it will have a right to veto it. If there are several of them, the verdict to be by a straight majority. That's democratic, isn't it?"

"In a way," said Mr Pocock. He wished he could dispose of the sherry, but if he drank it too quickly he was going to choke. "But one has to look at the other side of the coin. The new road will be a great benefit to a number of householders."

"Including you."

"Yes. It's true that my present house happens to be on that stretch of road. But I hope you don't impute—"

"I don't impute anything," said the colonel. "I state facts. Mine is the only property which is going to be invaded, and that means that I am the only person directly concerned."

He gazed out of the window. From where he stood he could see, across two fields, the line of hedge which marked the main road—a thick hedge of well-matured beech. What he now had to face was the thought of a road, a loathsome snake of tar macadam, giving right of access to every Tom, Dick, and Harry with a stinking motorcar or a roaring motorcycle, violating lands which had been in the Mounteagle family for two and a half centuries. Was it for this that they had fought Napoleon, Kaiser William, and Hitler, that one Mounteagle had fallen in the breach at Badajoz, and another in the sodden wastes of Passchendaele, that he himself—?

He looked down at his left hand from which three of the middle fingers were gone. Mr Pocock, not fancying the expression on his face, managed to swallow most of the sherry in his glass.

"It may not be easy to push such a bill through," said the colonel. "But it's a chance. And maybe your last chance to settle this matter without bloodshed."

"Metaphorically, I hope you mean," said Mr Pocock with a nervous smile.

"I'm not in the habit of talking in metaphors," said the colonel. "If you put me with my back to wall, I shall fight."

"And, oh dear," said Mr Pocock to his wife that evening, "I've got a feeling he meant it."

"You can't possibly promote an antisocial bill of that sort."

"If I did, it would be the end of me, politically. And it wouldn't get a second reading. It would be laughed out of Parliament, and me with it."

"In that case," said his wife, "what's the difficulty? You just say no."

"You didn't see his face," said Mr Pocock.

*

"When I was in India," said Mr Fortescue, "there was a saying that all sappers were mad, married, or Methodist. Colonel Mounteagle is a bachelor, and a staunch upholder of the Established Church."

"So he must be mad," said Mr Calder.

When Mr Fortescue, Manager of the Westminster Branch of the London and Home Counties Bank, wished to make contact with Mr Calder or Mr Behrens, both of whom lived in Kent, he would convey a message to them that their accounts were causing him concern. The precise form of the message indicated the gravity of the situation. On this occasion it had been of very moderate urgency, and directed to Mr Calder only.

"Madness is an imprecise term," said Mr Fortescue. He steepled the tips of his fingers and looked severely at Mr Calder over his glasses.

"If you mean, is he certifiably insane, the answer must be in the negative. But his conduct in recent months has been causing concern in certain quarters. A number of my people have, as you know, succeeded in establishing themselves in positions of some confidence in IRA cells in this country. One of my people has managed to become friendly with Michael Scullin."

Mr Calder knew that the people referred to were very brave men who took their lives into their hands every day of the year. He also knew that the systematic penetration of IRA groups was one of the ways in which bomb outrages were kept within manageable limits.

He said, "Scullin? He's their electronics expert, isn't he?"

"One of them. He specializes in detonation by remote control, and devices of that sort. He learned his trade in Russia."

"I'm surprised that we don't take steps to abate him."

"On the whole it is more useful to keep him under observation. It can produce surprising results—as it has on this occasion. It seems that recently he has been paid substantial sums of money by a certain Colonel Mounteagle for what I can only describe as a refresher course in the use of high explosive."

"A refresher course?"

"Certainly. As a young officer, in 1945, Mounteagle had a

considerable reputation. He was a member of the task force charged with clearing the mouth of the Schelde, and blowing up the submarine pens. They were jobs which had to be done against time, and this involved the acceptance of risks. There was a procedure by which unmanned barges filled with explosive could be directed into the underground pens and exploded. The danger lay in the variety of underwater devices which had first to be brought to the surface and dismantled. It was while he was engaged in this work that the colonel lost three fingers of his left hand—and gained an immediate DSO."

"He sounds quite a lad," said Mr Calder. "Do we know what is leading him to a renewed interest in the forces of destruction?"

"He is annoyed with the authorities for wishing to build a road across his park and with his local MP for failing to introduce a private bill to stop them."

Mr Calder thought for a moment that Mr Fortescue was joking, then realized that he was serious. He said, "What sort of reprisals do you think he might be intending?"

"He could be laying a number of booby traps in his park. Alternatively, or in addition, he may be planning to blow up the MP concerned, a Mr Pocock. Two nights ago Mr Pocock was awakened by mysterious noises. He telephoned the police. When they arrived they found that the door of his garage had been forced. From the garage an unlocked door leads into the house."

"I see," said Mr Calder. "The colonel sounds like a determined character. Perhaps Mr Pocock would be wise to press on with his bill."

Mr Fortescue said, "I think we must take a hand. The loss of an occasional Member of Parliament may not be a matter of concern, but we don't want some innocent bulldozer driver destroyed. I suggest you make yourself known to the colonel. His address is Mounteagle Hall, Higham. He is managing director of his own family firm, the Clipstone Sand and Gravel Company. It is on the river, north of Coohag. I will alert Behrens as to the position, but I imagine you will be able to handle this yourself."

*

Mr Calder's methods were usually simple and straightforward. On this occasion he put on his oldest clothes, armed himself with a fishing rod, and sat down to fish at a point outside the boundary fence of the Clipstone Sand and Gravel Company. Soon after he had started, a man came out of a gate in the fence and stood watching him. From his appearance and walk he was an ex-naval type, Mr Calder guessed. At this moment he succeeded in hooking a sizeable fish.

This served as a convenient introduction, and Mr Calder was soon deep in conversation with Chief Petty Officer Seward. He mentioned that he was putting up for a few days at the local pub. Seward agreed that the beer there was drinkable, and that he might be down there himself after work.

By ten o'clock that evening, in the friendly atmosphere of the saloon bar, Mr Calder learned a good deal about the Clipstone Sand and Gravel Company and its owner.

"He's all right," said Seward. "I mean, you don't find many like him nowadays. He knows what he wants, and he likes to get his own way, no messing about. But if he likes you, he'll do anything for you."

"And if he doesn't like you?"

"If he doesn't like you," said Seward with a grin, "you clear out quick. We had a chap once who set himself up as a sort of shop steward. Wanted to get us unionized. The colonel soon put a stop to it."

"How did he manage to do that?"

"Threw him in the river."

"I see," said Calder thoughtfully.

"I don't say he would have got away with it in the usual outfit, but we're more a sort of family business. All ex-service. We've even got our own fleet."

Mr Calder had seen the neat row of grey metal barges anchored to the jetty.

"Lovely jobs," said Seward. "Self-powered. One man can handle them easily. Built to ferry stuff ashore on the beaches at D-Day. Picked them up from the Crown Agents after the war. Most of our stuff—sand and aggregate, that is—goes up by river. And they bring back timber piling and iron sheeting. When we're

opening a new section of quarry we have to blanket off each
section as we go—"

He expounded the intricacies of the quarryman's job, and Mr
Calder, who always liked to learn about other people's work,
listened with interest.

He said to Mr Behrens when he met him three days later,
"Mounteagle's a real buccaneer. The sort of man who used to go
out to India in the seventeenth century and come back with a
fortune and a hobnailed liver. But he's running a very useful outfit,
and his men swear by him."

"Would he be capable of blowing up a Member of Parliament?"
said Mr Behrens.

"Think nothing of it. He chucked a shop steward into the
river."

On the following Sunday Mr Calder paid a visit, by appointment,
to the modest villa residence of Alfred Pocock, MP. It stood, with
five similar residences, on the far side of the road which skirted
Colonel Mounteagle's park. He found Mr Pocock at home, alone
and depressed. He said, "I've sent my wife away to stay with
her mother. She didn't want to go but I thought it would be
safer."

"Much safer," said Mr Calder. "I take it the explosives experts
have given your house a clean bill of health."

"They poked around with some sort of machine which reacts to
explosives. They didn't find anything."

"I expect it was just a reconnaissance. The colonel's a
methodical man."

"He's a public menace," said Mr Pocock indignantly. "I'm told
that the workmen who should have started on the new road a week
ago have refused to proceed without police protection."

"I'm not sure that policemen would be much use. What they
need is a military reconnaissance screen, armed with mine
detectors."

"Then the colonel should be arrested."

"And charged with what?"

Mr Pocock gobbled a bit, but could think of no answer to this.
Mr Calder said, "I suppose you couldn't make some sort of gesture.

Have this bill he wants printed, and given a first reading. Since you're convinced it wouldn't get any further, no real harm would be done."

"It would be the end of my political life."

"If I had to make a choice between the ending of my political life and the ending of my life, I know which alternative I would select. But then, I'm a natural coward."

Mr Pocock, his voice rising as it did when he was excited or alarmed, said, "It's a scandal. We should all be given the fullest possible protection against menaces of this sort. It's what we pay our rates and taxes for and we're entitled to expect it."

"Having me on your side," said Mr Calder, "is what you might call a tax bonus."

Mr Pocock was not appeased. He shook hands coldly when his visitor left. Mr Calder, also, was silent. He was reflecting that maybe the trouble with England was that it was run by people like Mr Pocock and not by people like Colonel Mounteagle.

His next objective was to meet the colonel. Since he could hardly march up to the front door and introduce himself, this was a question of manoeuvre and good luck. He was early afoot on Monday morning and found two young men with white poles, a steel tape, and a theodolite on the road verge just south of the manor's great gates—high columns, each surmounted by a stone eagle poised to swoop.

As he stopped to talk to them a car swept out of the entrance. The colonel, who was driving, spotted the men, pulled up, and got out. The men looked apprehensive. The colonel was smiling. He said, "Getting ready for the great day, lads?"

"That's right, Colonel."

"The day when the first bulldozer drives through my hedge."

"That won't be us, Colonel. That's not our job."

"Someone's got to drive it. Can't do it by remote control." A thought struck him. "Come to think of it," he said, "when I was doing a similar sort of job during the war, we *did* use remote control. But that was ships, not bulldozers. No. As I said, someone will have to drive it." The colonel's smile widened. "Give him a message from me, lads. What he'll need is not police protection. He'll need insurance for his widow."

The colonel swung round and seemed to notice Mr Calder for the first time. He said, "Are you in charge of this mob?"

"Certainly not," said Mr Calder. "I just happened to be passing."

"You don't look to me like someone who happened to be passing. You look to me like a spy. This is war. And you know what happens to spies in war." The smile appeared again. "They get shot."

It was the smile that convinced Mr Calder. The colonel was neither eccentric nor in any way admirable. Whether he was mad or not was a nice point. What was certain was that he was very dangerous.

"We put a tap on both telephones," said Mr Fortescue. "The one from the house and the one from the factory. We picked up an interesting exchange yesterday afternoon. The colonel was speaking to a young friend of his, also ex-Army, it seems. A man called David Cairns. Cairns is assistant manager at an open-cast coal site at Petheridge, above Reading. Their coal goes down by river to the power stations at Battersea and Rotherhithe."

"And the colonel is ordering coal?"

"He is ordering explosives. A ton of slurry explosive. Stable, but extremely powerful. It is used in open-cast mining. And in quarrying."

"So the colonel has a legitimate reason for ordering it?"

"Certainly. And used in small quantities, under careful control, it can be perfectly safe. When I asked one of our Home Office experts what the effect would be of detonating a ton of it, he said that no one in his senses would do such a thing. When I pressed him he said it would blow a crater, roughly the size of a football field, perhaps twenty foot deep."

Mr Calder started to say, "Is there any reason to suppose—" but Mr Fortescue interrupted him sharply. He said, "There were two further points. The colonel is fetching this load himself. He will take one of the barges upstream tomorrow. A run of nine to ten hours. The loading will be done when he arrives. He has also ordered a quantity of timber, which will be stowed on top of the explosive. To keep it firmly in position, he said. No doubt a wise precaution. He plans to spend the night on the boat and start back early the following morning. I think it would be a good idea if you supervised the shipment. But I confess I shall feel much happier when the whole of this particular cargo is safely stowed in the explosives store of the Clipstone Sand and Gravel Company."

"Me, too," said Mr Calder.

There was a jetty at Petheridge, connected by a private railway with the loading bay at the open-cast colliery. A concrete track ran alongside the line. The colonel, who must have made an early start, tied up at the jetty at four o'clock. Mr Calder, who had come by road and had not needed to hurry, was ensconced in a thicket of alder and nettles at the far end of the jetty.

He awaited developments with interest.

The timber arrived first, by rail. The explosive, packed in wooden boxes, followed in a lorry, driven by a youngish man with the stamp of a cavalry officer, whom the colonel greeted as David, and whom Mr Calder assumed to be Cairns.

The wooden boxes were manhandled by the train crew and lowered into the barge. Nobody seemed unduly worried by their explosive potential, but Mr Calder noticed that they were not treated roughly. Once they were safely stowed, a small crane was brought into operation and this was used to sling on board the timber baulks, which had evidently been cut to length and which fitted snugly over the boxes.

By the time the loading was finished, evening was closing in. The train clanked off, and the colonel said something which Mr Calder was too far away to hear but which seemed to be an invitation to Cairns to come on board. He had been squatting among the nettles for three hours without achieving anything except cramp. Nothing much would happen before the barge started downstream at first light. Mr Calder's ideas turned to a drink and dinner. He got stiffly to his feet. He could see Cairns and the colonel standing in the lighted bridge house. He eased his way along the jetty in the hope that he might pick up what they were saying.

What the colonel was saying was, "I bet you don't know what this box of tricks does."

Cairns said, "You lose your bet, Colonel. Almost the only interesting thing I did in the Army was the long electronics course I took at Rhyl. It's an automatic steerer. Come to think of it, that must have been the sort of thing you used when you were blowing up those submarine pens."

"Roughly the same apparatus," said the colonel. "Roughly. But it was a good deal more primitive in those days."

If Cairns had noticed the expression on the colonel's face, he might have cut short the conversation at this point. As it was, he had moved on to a second box that was beside the auto-steerer and linked to it. Peering down at it he said, "This looks like a repeater. What would you need a repeater for?"

He put out one hand to touch the dial. The colonel said, in the tone of voice he might have used to a recalcitrant subaltern, "Don't touch that."

Cairn's head jerked back. He seemed suddenly to realize that something was wrong.

He said, "Do you mean that this repeater's already set? What on earth are you playing at?"

"That's none of your business."

Cairns was getting angry too. He said, "It is my business. You've got enough of my explosive on this craft to blow a hole in the Home Counties. And you've got an automatic steerer linked to a pre-set repeater. Unless you're prepared to tell me what you're playing at, I think I ought to report this to the police."

"You'll do nothing of the sort," said the colonel calmly. "I'll have no Tresham here." His hand came out of his pocket with a gun in it.

Calder was close enough by now to hear this, but not close enough to stop what followed. His feet were on the gangplank when the colonel shot Cairns through the heart, caught him as he fell, and heaved him over the side of the bridge and into the river. Hearing Mr Calder coming up the iron steps on to the bridge he swung round and shot him, once in the head and once in the body, and threw him overboard as well.

Then he put the gun back into his pocket, turned about, and descended into the cuddy. He was breathing a little faster, but otherwise showed no particular sign of emotion. His hand, as he poured himself a whisky from a bottle in the bulkhead cupboard, was steady as a rock.

The first shot had creased Mr Calder, plowing a long furrow along the side of his head above the ear and rendering him temporarily unconscious. He had twisted as he fell, so that the second shot went into the right side of his chest, deflecting from the ribs and coming out under his right shoulder-blade.

The fall into the chilly November waters of the Thames brought him round. He could use his legs, and with difficulty, his left arm. He realized that he was losing blood fast.

He let himself go with the current, kicking feebly toward the right bank, because he remembered that the towpath was on that side.

An eternity of cold and increasing pain.

Then he felt himself grounding on the gravel foreshore. Above him was a low wall of what seemed to be concrete sacks. He realized that he was incapable of climbing it and getting out on to the towpath.

He lay on his back and shouted.

The first passer-by was a young girl. She took one look down at Mr Calder and scampered away. The next one, twenty interminable minutes later, was a policeman.

Mr Behrens reached Reading Infirmary just before midnight. He was shown into a bleak reception office where he kicked his heels for ten minutes. His temper was wearing thin when a young doctor came in, accompanied by a policeman whom Mr Behrens recognized—Superintendent Farr of the Reading police.

The superintendent said, "As soon as we knew it was Calder we got in touch with your office. They said, put the silencers on. Have you any idea what this is all about?"

"Why don't we ask Calder? He might be able to tell us."

"He won't tell you anything," said the doctor. Then he noted the expression on Mr Behren's face.

"Sorry," he said. "I didn't mean that. He's not dead yet, and with a bit of luck we'll keep him that way. But he's lost a lot of blood. And lying about on the river bank in this weather can't have helped. I've put him under, and he'll have to stay that way for the time being."

"How long will that be?"

"The longer the better for him," said the doctor.

Mr Behrens recognized the finality of this. He said to Farr, "Can *you* tell me anything? We're all of us totally in the dark. It may be important."

"All I can tell you is that one of my men found him, on the river bank, whistled up an ambulance, and got him in here. It was when they were going through his wallet that they found his 'I' card with the special instructions on it, and got hold of me."

"Did he say anything before you put him under? Anything at all?"

"Not really," said the doctor. "If I'd known it was going to matter I might have listened more carefully." Men who were brought in with two bullet wounds in them and were important enough to bring the head policeman round at midnight were something new in his experience. "He did mention two names, though—several times over. One was Cairns and the other, I think, was Tresham."

"Tresham?" said Mr Fortescue thoughtfully, when Mr Behrens spoke to him on the telephone. "I seem to remember a man of that name. Tresham or Trencham. He was a Norfolk fisherman. He gave a lot of help to German agents landing by submarine on the east coast."

"And was Calder involved?"

"He was at Blenheim at the time. He could have been."

"Then this might have nothing to do with Mounteagle. It might be a revenge killing. By Tresham's son perhaps."

"I don't think," said Mr Fortescue precisely, "that this is a case in which it would be wise to jump to conclusions. What about Cairns?"

"He's a bachelor. We've telephoned his digs. No answer. The police are sending a car round."

Mr Fortescue digested this news in silence for some seconds. Then he said, "I'll look into the Tresham case. And I'll arrange for the police to monitor Mounteagle's barge as it goes downstream tomorrow. There's a lot to do. I suggest you go home and get some sleep. Be at the bank by nine tomorrow morning."

Mr Behrens went back home to the Old Rectory in the sleepy Kentish village of Lamperdown, and he lay on his bed, but he did not go to sleep. The answer to a lot of their problems was under his hand, if only he could close his fingers on it.

The deceptive light of false dawn was in the sky, and the first cocks were beginning to crow across the valley when Mr Behrens got up, pulled on his dressing gown, and made his way downstairs, walking quietly, so as not to wake his aunt, who shared the house with him and was a light sleeper.

He switched on the reading lamp in his study and searched the shelves for the book he wanted. In the end he found it among a complete set of works of Charles Dickens.

"Are you suggesting," said Mr Fortescue, "that Colonel Mounteagle intends to blow up the Houses of Parliament?"

"That's right."

"And you found this in *A Child's History of England*?"

"It was the only book I could lay my hand on quickly," said Mr Behrens apologetically.

It was not yet six o'clock in the morning but Mr Fortescue was dressed in the pin-stripe trousers and black coat appropriate to a senior bank official. Also he had shaved, which was more than Mr Behrens had done. He turned his attention to the book and read it once again.

" 'Lord Mounteagle, Tresham's brother-in-law, was certain to be in the House; and when Tresham found that he could not prevail upon the rest to devise any means of sparing their friends, he wrote a mysterious letter to this Lord and left it at his lodging in the dusk, urging him to keep away from the opening of Parliament.' So Tresham has nothing to do with our Norfolk fisherman?"

"Nothing at all. Tresham is probably something Calder heard the colonel saying when he shot Cairns."

"Then you think Cairns is dead?"

"I'm afraid so."

"The whole thing is unthinkable. Totally unthinkable. And yet—"

Now that he was getting used to it, Mr Fortescue seemed to be finding the idea of the wholesale destruction of the legislature more interesting than shocking. "An outrageous idea. How would one set about it?"

"It's some sort of automatic pilot with a receiver at the other end to guide it."

"Then has something been planted in the House?"

"I fancy the receiver will be going there tonight. In Pocock's car. That would be what the colonel was up to when Pocock heard burglars."

"How could he be certain that Pocock would be there tonight?"

"It's the debate on Common Market finance. His pet subject. He'll be there early and stay late."

"Well, we can soon see if you're right. We'll call on Pocock. And we'll take Brackett with us. If he finds this gadget in Pocock's car, do you know, I shall be almost inclined to believe you."

"He could hardly have chosen a more appropriate day for it," said Mr Behrens. The calendar on Mr Fortescue's desk had not yet been turned from the previous day. It showed November 4th.

An hour later, as the milkman and the postman were delivering their wares, three men stood in Mr Pocock's garage and watched the fourth at work. Major Brackett, who looked like a dyspeptic bloodhound and was the top electronics expert in the Ministry of Defence, was lying on his back under the car. He said, "It's here all right. Wired on to one of the cross-members. A very neat job."

He eased his way out, stood up, and wiped a drop of oil from his nose.

"That's all right then," said Mr Fortescue. "All we have to do is switch it off." And when Brackett said nothing. "Well, isn't it?"

"I'm afraid not," said the major sadly. "Once this jigger's set and on beam, if you turn it off, or interfere with it in any way, you activate the switch at the other end, and your barge load goes up."

"I think, Major," said the Home Secretary, "that if you could explain, in terms simple enough to be understood by someone like myself who knows nothing about electronics, then we might be able to see our way more clearly."

Apart from Major Brackett, his audience consisted of the Police Commissioner, the head of the Special Branch, Commander Elfe, Chief Superintendent Baker in charge of River Division, and Mr Fortescue. Mr Behrens was sitting unobtrusively in the background.

"Well," said the major, "there are a number of different ways of detonating explosives at a distance."

"As we know," said Elfe grimly.

"The simplest is a pair of linked sets. Master and slave, we call them. The master emits an impulse which increases in strength as the two sets come together. When they are a predetermined distance apart the stonger 'kills' the weaker one. This throws a switch, and the explosive goes up."

"I'm with you so far," said the Home Secretary.

"It can be linked to an automatic steering device. We've developed one recently, on the ranges at Bovington. It steers an old tank filled with explosive into an enemy strong point and detonates it when it gets there. In fact, if Mounteagle has managed to get hold of the latest box of tricks, there's an additional jigger which not only keeps the tank on a predetermined course but allows it to side-step obstacles. It's done with an 'eye'—a photocell connected with a microprocessor that registers changes of light striking the cell and takes the appropriate action."

"Does that means that Mounteagle need never go on board at all? Suppose he's fixed the slave set to go off at—what? Fifty yards? That would be about the distance from the edge of the embankment to the car park under the House. Then he could leave it to steer itself downstream."

"I doubt he'd do that," said Baker. "The barge would call too much attention to itself, zigzagging down the river like a pinball. He'll surely take it down as far as he can by manual steering—at least until it's dark. Any time after that, I agree, he could leave it to its own devices."

For a moment the men in the room were silent. They were watching a steel craft, packed with enough explosive to tear the top off a mountain, sliding downstream in the darkness, steering under bridges, avoiding other boats, obedient only to the beckoning of its master in Parliament.

The Home Secretary said, "Where is it now?"

The Commissioner said, "Our last report was Bell View Lock below Runnymede. The colonel was certainly on board then. He was making about four miles an hour." He was studying a map that Baker had produced. "Say it's dark by seven. If he keeps up that speed he'd be ten miles above Westminster by then."

"The tide'll be against him when he gets below Teddington," said Baker. "He won't make more than three miles an hour after that."

Everyone did some mental arithmetic.

Elfe said, "Then H-hour could be either side of ten o'clock."

"Is there any chance," said the Home Secretary, "of getting someone aboard *after* the colonel's left and reverting to—what did you call it?—manual steering."

"If you tried that," said Brackett, "you'd almost certainly send the whole lot up. No. I'm afraid there's only one answer. Put the master set from Pocock's car into a police launch and lead the barge out to sea. Safe enough if the launch keeps two hundred yards ahead. Have an experienced man in charge."

"I'll take it myself," said Baker. "That is," he added with a grin, "if the major will come with me in case of any—er—technical hitches."

"I was afraid you were going to say that," said Brackett, looking sadder than ever.

"Very well, gentlemen," said the Home Secretary briskly. "That seems to be the best plan. You have total authority to clear the river of craft, and take any other precautionary measures you think necessary. I assume that Mounteagle plans to bolt abroad. You'll take the usual steps to block the exits."

The Commissioner said, "It occurs to me, Home Secretary, that if we succeed in taking the barge out to sea and destroying it, we shall have very little real evidence left. Suppose he decides to brazen it out."

"He'll have to brazen out one murder and one attempted murder," said Mr Fortescue coldly. "Calder recovered sufficiently an hour ago to tell us what happened at Petheridge."

"When you're dealing with a madman," said the Home Secretary, "it's impossible to predict what he'll do."

Mr Behrens disagreed, though he felt it was hardly his place to

say so. He thought he knew exactly what the colonel was planning
to do.

At ten o'clock that night Mr Behrens was sitting, alone, on a bench
on a hilltop on the northern fringe of London. In front of him, and
below him, a million lights twinkled through the misty darkness.
There were smaller lights, which were windows and lamp
standards and motorcars, and larger lights which were bonfires.
The nearest was a quarter of a mile below the point where he was
sitting. He could see the dark figures congregated round it like
priests at a ritual burning, and he could see, lashed to a stake on
top, the grotesque parody of Guy Fawkes, the first great
pyrotechnic.

A rocket sailed up into the sky and burst in clusters of red and
yellow lights.

Mr Behrens had chosen this particular place because he had
remembered something Mr Calder had once told him and he was
convinced that Colonel Mounteagle, if he avoided immediate
capture, would come there too.

A bronze plaque, set in a stone pillar beside the bench, was the
reason for his certainty.

"Parliament Hill Fields," it said, "so named because the
conspirators who, in the year 1605, planned to blow up the Houses
of Parliament, escaping to the north, halted their horses at this
spot to observe the outcome of their device."

With his strong sense of history, the colonel must surely come
to that spot to observe the outcome of his own more powerful and
sophisticated device.

Mr Behrens was wondering exactly what the colonel had
planned to do, and what he would have done but for the
unfortunate contretemps at Petheridge. There were several ways in
which he might have escaped detection. On the supposition that
the original barge would be destroyed beyond any possibility of
identification, he needed only to have a duplicate ready filled with
explosive, of which he had no doubt already accumulated a stock
at his works, waiting for him below Tower Bridge. He could then
proceed quietly on his way with this and turn a bland face of
innocence to the world. Suspicion, yes. But proof would turn on a

number of imponderables, such as whether they could prove the acquisition by the colonel of the self-steering device.

It was at this moment that Mr Behrens heard a car draw up and stop on the road above him. A door slammed. Footsteps came crunching down the cinder track towards the seat. Mr Behrens had never met the colonel, but he had been shown photographs of him, and in the dying light of the rocket he had no difficulty in recognizing him.

The colonel stood for a long minute, in silence, staring down at the scene below. Mr Behrens stood up, and the movement caught the colonel's eye. He turned his head.

"A magnificent spectacle, is it not?" said Mr Behrens.

The colonel grunted.

"But I fear that the main attraction has been cancelled. Owing, you might say, to a technical hitch. When it does take place, it will be some miles offshore, and with a very limited audience."

The colonel was motionless, a black figure outlined against the night sky. When he spoke his voice sounded quite easy. He said, "Who are you, little man?"

"I doubt if this is really a moment for introductions," said Mr Behrens. "I am a very old friend of one of the men you shot last night. Not Cairns, the other one."

"The Government spy."

"I suppose that's as good a description as any."

"And what do you propose to do about it?"

The colonel had swung round now, but both his hands were visible, hanging by his side. Mr Behrens moved toward him until he was quite close, watching the colonel's hands all the time.

He said, "It seemed to me that there was only one logical end to this matter, Colonel. You come up here to witness the success of your plan. Being disappointed in its failure—we may assume by now, I think, that it has failed—you decide to take your own life."

So saying, Mr Behrens shot Colonel Mounteagle neatly through the heart. He had removed the silencer from his gun, being confident that the noise of the shot would arouse no interest on this particular night. He stooped over the crumpled body, pressed the muzzle against the entry point of the bullet, and fired again.

Then he wiped the gun carefully and pressed it into the colonel's right hand.

A salvo of rockets soared up into the sky, and burst almost overhead with a loud crack and a shower of silver rain.

THE NOTIF

Madelaine Duke

Dear Val,

I don't need reminding that you are my twin sister and I know
that we are hypersensitive to one another. And I would have
written to you sooner if I hadn't put off telling Ian. Somehow I
didn't relish it, but last night I came out with it. I just told him that
I'd seen a gynaecologist.

He looked at me across the dinner table. "Whatever for?"

I said, "I wanted to know whether there's anything wrong with
me."

"Why should anything be wrong?"

"We have been married four years and we're still childless."

"Anna, keep your voice down." He looked around the little
bar–restaurant. "This is no place for discussing such things."

Where else? If I'd raised the subject at home he would have
found some reason for going out.

I told him, "The specialist says there is no reason why I
shouldn't have children. My inside is perfectly normal."

"All right, Anna, all right. I never said it wasn't. What's the
hurry all of a sudden? Give it time."

"We have given it time. Long enough according to the specialist.
What he suggested is that it's you, Ian, who should consult
someone who deals with fertility problems."

"I have no problems."

"Ian, there might be some slight abnormality, something that
can be treated. Please will you go and see someone about it?"

"No."

"Just . . . no?"

"Look here, Anna. You seem to have forgotten what my
profession is."

I asked him, "How much do you know about the body below the neck?"

"More than you do."

"I am not medically trained."

"Good of you to admit it, Anna. Now we're almost there."

Where? I wondered whether it was something Ian said to his patients just before his drill hit a nerve.

"I am a dental surgeon. Right?" Ian put on his patient face. "Has it not occurred to you that I had to learn a lot of medicine before I could qualify? Take physiology . . ."

I didn't want to take physiology. What for? I know Ian's technique of turning any subject into a pseudo-academic lecture.

"Listen, Ian," I pleaded. "We've got to talk . . ."

"Like adults?" He smiled with his beautiful teeth. "That's what you were going to say."

"I was not."

"It doesn't matter, Anna. Finish your coffee and let's go. I'll have a busy day tomorrow."

The waitress would have brought him the bill, but he got up and went to the cash desk. End of non-discussion. Escape.

Ian couldn't have escaped—at least, not physically—on the drive home. I was tempted to try again. Surely it would be sensible to seek medical advice. After all, he had been the one who'd wanted us to buy a house big enough for children. In the end I asked myself what my sister would do. We both know, don't we, Val? I kept my mouth shut.

So, dear Val, here's my blow-by-blow "he said, she said" report. What next? I don't know but it won't be evening classes for boiled pudding cookery.

As ever,
Anna

Dear Val,

Your cutting from the *Financial Times* was not only interesting because I used to work for the Masterson Company. It gave me an idea for the future. I cleared out the big room in the attic and converted it into a studio. Then I spent a month working out new textile and wallpaper designs. But I didn't have to labour. There seemed to be no end to the colours, shapes and images in my head. When I'd completed a whole range I phoned London and made an appointment with Mr Carson. He used to be Masterson's sales director. He's the chairman now.

Back to the bit in the *Financial Times*. I guessed that Masterson's had made a generous offer for the Marc Bernais Company in order to acquire Bernais' raw-material supplies, Spanish cotton, and the factories in France. In fact, Masterson's were planning considerable expansion and would be in the market for new designs.

My appointment with Mr Carson turned into a business lunch with the Board of Directors. What luxury! Outside London was sweltering, but we were in an air-conditioned, soundproof dining room above the executive suite, eating the most delicious salads and cold meats, drinking vintage Montrachet. At the end of it I was back in business, not as a poor free-lance whose designs may or may not be bought but as Masterson's chief designer. In the train back to Brighton I was in a state of euphoria. It lasted as far as Haywards Heath, and then I began to worry about Ian's reaction to my news.

I got home about half-past five. Ian wouldn't be back for another hour or more. I changed into cotton trousers and a shirt and walked down to the beach. There was less breeze than usual and the sea licked the shingle lazily, like a mother cat washing her kittens. The moist pebbles shimmered in shades of slate-grey and blue, white and pale gold. The shifting patterns of stone suggested an original print on glazed chintz. Out at sea something was moving towards the shore. A dolphin in the English Channel? Surely not. But it was too small for a dinghy.

Some twenty minutes later the thing became recognizable as a swimmer, a fourteen- or fifteen-year-old boy with a tanned body and black hair. He made the beach in a beautiful gliding sweep.

"Have you seen a red towel?" he asked me.

I said I had, some way up.

He walked along beside me. "I thought there was a bit of a current."

"You've been a long way out. Isn't that rather dangerous?"

"Not for me. I got my gold life-saving medal last month." The dolphin-boy was a child after all.

"All the same, perhaps you shouldn't go so far on your own."

"Come with me tomorrow."

"I can't swim."

"Why not?"

"I suppose I can . . . a bit. But I'm scared in water."

"I know what you mean. I used to be scared because, when I was little, I nearly drowned. Is that what happened to you?"

"Something like it," I told him. "Someone dived on top of me."

He looked me up and down. "What's your name?"

"Anna."

"I am Patrice."

"French?"

"Mongrel. My mother is French, my father comes from Morocco, but I was born in London. Anna, do you want to be able to swim?"

"Yes. My husband is a good swimmer."

"All right, I'll teach you." We had found his towel. He put it on like a Roman toga. "I'll meet you here at five tomorrow."

"Patrice, I don't know . . ."

But he was off, racing over the stones as if they were made of cotton wool.

Val dear, I didn't have time to finish this letter last night. When I got home Ian asked where I'd been all day. He'd phoned twice, he'd wanted to arrange dinner with the Fergusons. I apologized and told him I'd been in London. He asked why I didn't tell him.

"I don't really know," I admitted. "I suppose I don't like talking about vague plans. But they're not vague any more. I've landed a wonderful job . . . chief designer at Masterson's."

He got up and helped himself to a sherry. "In London, I suppose."

"About three days a week. I'll be able to do a lot of the work at home."

"So it's all settled . . . behind my back."

"Ian, I didn't expect such an offer. I didn't think for a moment . . ."

"No, you didn't think." His mouth got small and pinched in. He was speaking quietly through his teeth. Well, you know how he looks when he is displeased. "You don't think. That's the most typical thing about you. I don't suppose you considered our social life. You should know by now that one doesn't build up a successful private practice without the right contacts. And what about my income tax? If your job is that important it'll put up our joint earnings; most of your money will go in tax . . ."

I said his earnings would go up too if I concentrated on the social rat-race for him and built up the private side of his practice.

He tossed back another sherry. "I wish you wouldn't argue about things you don't understand. My accountant . . ."

Even I know that a good accountant can drastically reduce one's income tax. It's a subject I've listened to often enough at his colleagues' cocktail parties.

But enough of that. By the time we got into bed I felt exhausted. Ian went to sleep as soon as his head hit the pillow. After a while I managed to shut out all but a couple of sensations, going to do the work I enjoy and going into the sea with Patrice.

Dear Val, you can stop worrying about me.

Anna

Dear Val,

I've discovered the pleasures of fresh air all over again. London is sticky and stinks of petrol fumes, but when I get home to Brighton the roses in our garden seem more fragrant than ever and the salt air on the beach is a joy. If the hot weather lasts a bit longer I'll become quite confident in the sea.

Patrice is a wise child. He never urges me to go further than I want and he always stays close to me. He dives under me and circles around like a dolphin at play yet never disrupts the rhythm I am gradually developing. We now go to another beach where there are few bathers, near Portslade. I don't want Ian to hear that I'm learning to swim; anyway not yet. I don't quite know why, except that I am afraid that he might discourage me. I'm as easily put off as you are. Deep down we're timorous.

Ian's sister Maggie is spending the week with us. On Saturday morning it was so hot that even Maggie wanted a swim. Ian said very firmly that it was no use asking me to go with them because I was still scared stiff of water, I had "a thing" about it. He suggested I make a picnic and take it down to the beach later. That's what I did.

Patrice was there by himself, as usual. Since Maggie's been here I hadn't had time to meet him. While we were eating he went far out to sea, something he never does when we are on our own. After his swim he played with a ball, heading and dribbling it until even Ian noticed his skill. Then Ian caught the ball and they played together.

Maggie looked proud of her brother. "You know," she said, "Ian played soccer at school. He was very good."

Ian was remembering that too. He was giving instructions to the boy, showing him how to play like a professional, looking pathetically clumsy compared with Patrice. My young friend listened to Ian politely, but he soon wandered off.

Ian remembered that he'd fixed up a game of golf for himself and Maggie, so the two of them took off. While I cleared up the picnic Patrice returned.

He squatted beside me. "Why didn't you swim?"

"I don't know."

"Was that your husband?"

"Yes."

"He's what I imagined. He looks all right, but . . ."

"Well?"

"You make me think of my sister." It was the first time he'd mentioned her. I'd seen him as an only child. "Claudine was married . . ."

Was. I dared not ask Patrice about her. He looked sad.

He brushed the hair out of his eyes. "Funny . . . your husband is like Claudine's. We had a name for people like him. *Notif*."

"Is that French?"

He smiled. "No. It was our private name for Denis. *Notif* . . . no taste, no imagination, no feelings. You know . . ."

Devastating. I didn't know what to think or to say. Eventually I did ask him why he had such a poor opinion of my husband. It wasn't as if I'd discussed Ian with him. I wouldn't discuss Ian with anyone except you, least of all with a child.

Patrice even looked very young while he thought how to answer my awkward question. "I don't really have an opinion about your husband. It's just a sort of feeling . . ." He picked up a flat pebble and sent it skimming over the water. "But your husband is a Notif, isn't he?"

As ever,
Anna

Dear Val,

What a fuss about a holiday! But it's all settled now. Ian wanted out of rainswept Brighton, but insisted that he wouldn't go abroad without me, much as he needed the break. I really think he was hoping that Masterson's would dismiss me for requesting time off so soon after starting the job. Who would want a chief designer run by her man?

However, by working late hours I managed to get the new designs fabric-tested and ready for production. And Carson was pleasant about giving me three weeks off.

This time Ian has made all the travel arrangements. And there's an innovation. We're going with another couple. Andrew Ferguson is the president of the Caledonian Society, Jenny is a doctor at the Children's Hospital. It was Jenny who told me about infertility problems. You may remember Jenny. We had lunch together last time you were in England. She gave you the book on identical twins.

Jenny was amusing about Ian organizing our holiday. She told me everybody who was anybody knew that poor Ian had to make all the arrangements himself because his wife was too busy professionally . . . top job in industry, unique for a woman. Had I lost my job, said Jenny, Ian would have put it about that poor Anna had been unable to cope but that the job was unimportant as Anna has a husband who looks after her.

Jenny was a little bitchy but right. It's strange how predictable Ian has become to me since Patrice introduced me to the Notif's character. While I took down our suitcases last night I knew what would happen and felt as if I'd lived the coming hour over and over again. Ian put out the clothes he wanted me to pack for him. What a jumble! Cream trousers, white shirts, a green sweater, black shoes.

I said, "These things don't go together."

"Why not?" he snapped.

"Perhaps your cream shirt would look better with the cream trousers."

"Have it your way. What else is wrong?"

"Nothing's wrong. I just wondered whether you couldn't take colours that fit in with each other."

"Such as?"

"How about your beige shoes instead of the black, and the beige sweater . . . not the green."

He took the beige sweater from the shelf and threw it on the bed. "It's dirty. All right, all right, I should have put it in your laundry. But I had more important things on my mind."

"I'll wash it."

"It won't dry by morning . . . Damn! I can't take these trousers either. The zip's broken."

"Sorry, Ian."

"You might have noticed it when you took them to the cleaner's. But there isn't much you notice these days. Too preoccupied with high life in London. For heaven's sake, do your own packing and let me get on with mine."

In the end he complained that he couldn't get his suitcase shut. So, while he was having a bath, I repacked it and it closed easily.

What fun we had when you and I travelled together. No great preparations. We just went when we could, where we could. I'd better go to bed now. We're off at dawn. Ian should be asleep by now. By the way, I couldn't find Minturno on our maps either. Ian got the name from a patient who told him Minturno was a lovely, unspoiled headland on the west coast north of Naples. I suppose the place does exist. I'll let you know from Italy.

Good night,
Anna

Dear Val,

You would like Minturno. It's very different from the seaside resorts Ian used to pick for our holdiays, just a white village perched above a rocky bay. Our hotel is a traditional *locanda* with a vine-covered pergola. There is no casino, no disco, no smart restaurant. Evenings we sit under the grapes, drink the local wine and talk.

The Fergusons are good company. While Ian and Andrew swop golf stories—there seems to be no end of them—Jenny and I talk about people and places and paintings. Jenny is a knowledgeable amateur art-historian. We have more in common than I expected.

The days are hot and sunny and we are spending them on the beach. We have found a sandy cove almost surrounded by rocks that shimmer like jewels. Big chunks of them are veined with bands of clear crystal. I've never seen such beautiful stones.

When I walked into the sea the day after we arrived—I was the first to go in—Ian told me I'd better remember that I can't swim. I said I'd been learning.

"Don't be silly. A few lessons in a public swimming-pool. You've done it before and it didn't get you anywhere."

Jenny got up and joined me. "Come on, Anna. Let's go."

The water was translucent and green, like inexpensive glass, and much warmer than the sea at Brighton. Jenny stayed with me until she was convinced that I was all right and then went back on the sands. I swam out about fifty yards. For a moment the old fear made me feel nauseated, but for a moment only. In the distance a shining black rock kept dipping in and out of the water; it looked like a dolphin that had come to play with me. No more doubts. I was in my element.

When I got back Ian said, "I told you often enough, you'll never make a swimmer until you change your attitude."

"I *have* changed my attitude," I assured him.

Before I understood the nature of the Notif I would have tried to explain to Ian *what* changed my attitude. I'd have tried earnestly, too earnestly perhaps, out of a desire to share the experience with him. Not a world-shaking experience, just a child's gifts of kindness and confidence. Now I know how futile it would be to tell Ian about Patrice. He'd assume that I'd been paying for the lessons and tell me I was mad to allow a cocky kid to take advantage of me.

I've had a letter from Patrice. He says, "I found your place in Italy. It is a dot on an old map that used to belong to my sister. What is the sea like where you are? You really are OK now, but be careful. Every sea is different. Claudine was a super swimmer. I think I should tell you. She drowned. In Italy. In the Med. Denis was in the water with her. They said it was an accident."

Love,
Anna

Dear Val,

Two more days and we'll be back in the English autumn. Last night Ian remembered that he'd been missing out on a habitual feature of our holidays—more sex than at home. He's a bit tired. It must be years since he's been swimming so much. I don't know what's possessing him; however far I swim he must overtake me. But perhaps I do know. I've gone more than halfway to the black rock, the one shaped like a dolphin, and he doesn't like it. It's as if he felt that I am threatening his supremacy.

After dinner, last night, he asserted himself. He kept stroking me—arms, shoulders, thighs—until Andrew and Jenny couldn't fail to note that we were about to indulge in marital bliss. Ian certainly indulged. He bit my neck and shoulder where it would show, ground his unshaven face into mine and pounded me with all his weight. It was even worse than usual because I was afraid he'd be unable to complete the act, which would put him in a bad mood for the rest of the holiday. However, after a lot of hard breathing he achieved his satisfaction and rolled off me.

It seemed the right moment for an intimate talk. I asked him whether he had seen a specialist about "our" infertility problem.

"What for?" he asked. "You don't want a family. You've got the ideal job."

"That's no alternative," I told him.

"I didn't say it was. Look here, Anna, I don't mind not having children. If you want my opinion . . . you've always been a career woman at heart. I've had to face it. I think you should face it too. Be honest with yourself."

How honest?

As ever,
Anna

Dear Val,

Thank you for your letter of November 10th. It was only natural for Andrew and me to do what we could. During the holiday we had come to appreciate your sister more than ever. Such a sweet, gentle girl.

The newspaper version of the accident has been nasty, but don't let it alarm you. One must see it for what it is. Basically the English reporter, just another holiday-maker, was after a sensational story. To me that was obvious at the time.

The man told the Italian police that he'd seen the whole thing from his hired boat. Andrew and I were on the beach, neither of us exactly watching. But we noticed Anna go in for a swim, Ian following her a little later. We paid no attention until we heard the shouting. It came from a fishing boat near the black rock.

Andrew and I made a point of telling the Italian police that the reporter did not arrive at the rock until well after the fishermen. But he kept insisting that he got to the scene at almost the same time. Fortunately the newspaperman overplayed his hand. Even the police were appalled at his accusation that Anna had sat on the rock and calmly watched Ian drown without lifting a finger. It was almost as if he were out to prove that she had egged Ian on to swim until he was exhausted. Ridiculous. One only needs to look at Anna to reject such an idea. The Italians did both.

Thank heavens the case is closed. Anna has taken our advice to do nothing about the newspaper story. Ignoring the innuendos will be the most effective way of killing them. Anna is coping well and even better since you told her that you will be here by Christmas.

Yours sincerely,
Jenny

THE FINGER OF SUSPICION

Tony Wilmot

THE DRAB, SPARSELY furnished room was like every other police "interview" room Tom had known: desk, half a dozen chairs, water-cooler and a telephone. Its sparseness was calculated; its purpose to intimidate a suspect, then to break him. A Y-shaped fan turned slowly overhead, barely moving the stale air. How many poor unfortunates, Tom wondered, had had their last breath of liberty in there?

It was ten a.m. Already the desert sun's rays, piercing through the window blind, made Tom uncomfortably hot. The heat in the Persian Gulf was something he had never completely adapted to.

Two plain-clothes men, jackets off, shirts open, sat behind the desk. One invited Tom to sit. The man's voice was pure Harvard. Late twenties, Tom judged. Ruthless ambition personified. The other man had heavy jowls, gimlet eyes and a world-weary expression. Less ambitious, Tom decided, but just as ruthless.

Tom rested his hands on his knees, hoping he looked at ease. The local Arab police had arrested him the night before. They had been most apologetic. It wasn't their doing, they'd said—an extradition order from the USA. They had no choice but to comply with it.

In his mind's eye, Tom could see Soraya's worried expression as she had answered the doorbell in the small hours: an Arab inspector and constable. *Tom, you promised me you'd given up your old way of life.* Tom had kept his promise; she must believe that. *Then what do the police want with you, Tom?* Nothing, he'd said; obviously it was a mistake. *They were confusing him with someone else.* Anything to reassure her and give himself time to think. *But why do they talk of extradition? Doesn't that mean you will have to go back to America?* Tom didn't have a convincing answer to that.

The local police chief withdrew, closing the door as he left. Heavy-jowls opened a dossier on the desk-top and began to read aloud.

"Thomas Bradley, aged thirty-two, born Hartford, Connecticut . . ." He went on to list Tom's various employments since quitting high school, ending with ". . . last known occupation, chauffeur. Right so far, Bradley?"

Tom nodded. Let them do all the talking.

"What isn't included in your personal file, Bradley, are your, shall we say, extra-curricular activities—such as your penchant for petty larceny . . ."

The word "penchant" caught Tom's attention. An odd word for a tough, world-weary FBI man to be using. Deep down, he'd always been expecting the FBI to catch up with him. He'd never confided that to Soraya: she would have only worried herself sick. And even if she suspected there were things in his past he would sooner forget about, she had never said.

Something else was bothering Tom. The way Heavy-jowls' sidekick was listening, observing, making mental notes. There was something about the man that was very un-cop-like, more like a psychologist.

The grilling went on. Tom answered obliquely. Why volunteer information? But as the minutes slipped by, Tom became more uneasy; their method of questioning was like nothing he had known before—elliptic and full of subtle innuendo.

Suddenly the younger one said, "You think we're *cops*, Bradley?" He made it sound like a four-letter word.

"Well, aren't you?" Tom felt cold inside . . . the Harvard accent, their unorthodox style, their beautifully tailored suits . . . the pieces were beginning to fall into place.

"We're not Police Department amateurs, Bradley. We're CIA."

Tom had been into petty larceny, from leaving high school until his mid-twenties. The police had pulled him in a few times but could never get enough evidence to make a charge stick, releasing him with the usual veiled threats. He had been lucky. But he knew it was only a matter of time before they nailed him, so he decided to go straight. After a year or two, the police lost interest in him.

Tom took a training course as a chauffeur. He'd always been able to handle a car well, and he had the clean-cut looks that went with a uniform.

His first employment was as driver to the owner of a computer hardware firm. The man lived on Long Island. Tom found the work enjoyable, but the man's wife, riddled with complexes over having been born in the Bronx, was forever ordering him to drive her to Bloomingdale's or Macy's; forever castigating him for "dumb insolence"; for "getting us into traffic snarl-ups"; for "not treating me like a lady".

His patience finally snapped—and he then quit. The computer man was sorry to lose him and gave him a glowing reference.

He had had a string of jobs after that. Then, one day, he got a call from his old boss, the computer man. A friend, government brass in Washington, was looking for a chauffeur. Was Tom available?

Tom made a favourable impression on the Washington man, a Mr Brodie, who said he would be in touch, but Tom heard nothing for a month. Then Mr Brodie's secretary rang: could Tom come in for a final interview?

Mr Brodie had looked distinctly embarrassed, Tom thought. He explained that something had been bothering him; perhaps Tom could straighten things out? A security check had revealed that Tom had once been under suspicion with the New York PD in connection with some robberies.

Tom had lied through his teeth. Not only had he not had anything to do with the crimes, he assured Mr Brodie, but he had filed a complaint for wrongful arrest and police harassment (he hadn't, but he knew it would be impossible for the NYPD to refute it).

Mr Brodie had been all smiles. He had been sure that the answer would be no, but he had had to hear it from Tom's own lips. Now, how soon could Tom start?

Mr Brodie had an office in the National Security Agency. Everyone, even the senior staff, was on Christian name terms. Tom was surprised at the informality—"But it must always be 'sir' when we're outside the office, Tom"—but he liked the atmosphere. The work was not too taxing and Mr Brodie was a pleasant man, easy to get along with. It was not long before Tom discovered that Brodie was cheating on his wife; but Tom decided it was no concern of his.

For months the chauffeuring went smoothly. Then, off duty, Tom met a stunning girl in a singles-bar. Her name was Charlene. Twenty-eight, a failed actress, a failed wife, but determined to make a financial killing before she lost her looks.

She regarded Tom as a one-night stand—until she learned who he was working for. She had a mental file on every VIP in Washington. In her book, Brodie was *hot property*. Somebody who handled top-secret data.

She had an apartment big enough for two, so why didn't Tom move in with her? (Tom could not move out of his rat-trap room fast enough!)

Night after night, the post-coital pillow-talk came around to the same theme: *Tom* had access to Classified data . . . *Charlene* had access to a buyer . . .

"You listening to us, Bradley?"

Tom's thoughts were jerked back to the present.

The Harvard-voiced sidekick went on, "You've got a cosy set-up here, Bradley. Shacked up with one of the local oil sheikhs' wives. Risky, pal, risky. They're pretty severe on adultery here, aren't they? You and she could get fifty lashes for that."

"The sheikh divorced her," Tom said. "We're married now."

The sidekick laughed softly; even his laugh had a Harvard sound. "Well, the honeymoon, as they say, is over. You'll be flying back to the States with us just as soon as the extradition papers are ready." He paused. "Does your new wife know you turned traitor, Bradley? No, I guess she doesn't. Couldn't bring yourself to tell her. Can't say I blame you. I'd be the same. It's a helluvan admission."

Icy ripples ran up Tom's spine. He felt numb with shock. They must have broken Charlene. How else could they have found out?

"Know what puzzles *me*, Bradley?" said Heavy-jowls, who had identified himself as Powers. "You could have gone to South America . . . the Islands . . . the South of France . . . Australia.

Yet you chose this Middle Eastern oil state. A place that's *dry*, for
God's sake!"

Tom's reason had been blind panic. He had never experienced
real fear before. Everything had suddenly crowded in on him. He
had not been able to eat or sleep or think.

In the beginning, getting data out of Mr Brodie's office had been
something of a caper. He had read spy stories, and had always
expected the real thing to be so much more difficult. But it couldn't
have been easier. Files labelled *Top Secret* or *Confidential* were left
lying around the office; and, often, when Mr Brodie was in
meetings and Tom was waiting in the Cadillac outside, Tom could
read Defence memoranda in Mr Brodie's many briefcases, as often
as not left unlocked.

Charlene had bought a microcamera for him to use in Mr
Brodie's office, but crazily, he'd never needed it. All he'd had to
do was photocopy the papers when Mr Brodie's secretary was out
to lunch. The camera would have shown up on the personnel body
scan, but the papers, hidden under his shirt, didn't.

It was all so simple. Charlene passed the info on to her contact
(Tom never asked his nationality, preferring not to have his
suspicions confirmed) and the money flowed in. Within a few
months Tom's share amounted to 10,000 dollars.

Tom had wanted to stop then, to quit while they were ahead, but
Charlene would not hear of it. To her, they had only scratched the
surface.

Her contact was willing to pay 20,000 dollars for a copy of a file
containing NATO intelligence-gathering activities. If Tom pulled
that one off, *then* he could quit.

Weeks passed but Tom never even saw the file. He began to
doubt its existence. Perhaps Mr Brodie was not as top-level as they
had thought? Tom had suggested, when Charlene's patience
finally ran out.

It was the first time she had ever threatened him. He'd better lay
his hands on that file—or else! Or else what? Tom wanted to know.
Would Charlene be ruthless enough to betray him?

He decided she probably would.

He renewed his efforts, riffling through Mr Brodie's briefcases at every opportunity. He found nothing that mentioned NATO's intelligence network.

Then, unexpectedly, Mr Brodie called him up to the office one morning, and handed him some files from the safe to take down to the car. In a cellophane folder, Tom saw what he had been looking for. He had felt sick with excitement. He knew Mr Brodie trusted him implicitly; now he could use that trust like a tool.

Tom's instructions were to drive his boss to his home near Annapolis, first stopping at an address on the outskirts of Washington—Mr Brodie's mistress's apartment. (Two afternoons a week, Tom would drop his boss off there, find a parking spot a few blocks away and read the paper for an hour before returning.)

He watched Mr Brodie disappear into the apartment block, then drove to a nearby shopping mall. He left his chauffeur's jacket and cap in the car, changed some dollar bills, then went to the public library. It took him exactly ten minutes to photocopy the file, page by page. He hid the copies under the plastic lining of the boot of the car.

And on the hour, Tom—the likeable, good-looking, utterly trustworthy Thomas Bradley—drove back to collect Mr Brodie.

But Tom's euphoria was short-lived. Their buyer wanted to talk to Tom, to reassure himself that the file copies were genuine. Tom thought it too risky, but Charlene was insistent. He must talk to the man or the deal was off.

For two nights he didn't sleep. Matters came to a head when Charlene told him, "Either you see him with me, Tom, or we're finished. And by that I mean *finished*. Period. I'll blow the whistle on you so loud it'll be like Watergate all over again."

Tom would never have known the man was not American born. Accent, mode of speech and behaviour, sense of humour—all were pure American. And all the time they talked, in an unfashionable bar, Tom had never once felt like a traitor. Why, the guy could have been a family friend!

It was only later, in the cold light of day, that he realized he was in deep water. If a security leak was discovered, wouldn't he be the obvious suspect?

In a blind panic, he had drawn out his savings and flown to London. From there to Kuwait. Nobody would think of looking for him on the Persian Gulf, he knew. He could pose as an American oil technician until he found work. But as he had drifted from one oil state to another, his dollars had melted at an alarming rate. That was when he met Soraya. She had hired him as her chauffeur–bodyguard, and very soon extended his duties in a most delightful way.

Powers lit a cigarette and leaned back in his chair. He tapped the dossier with a well-manicured fingernail.

"It says here, Bradley, that you run a small nightclub . . ."

"Yes," Tom said. "I gave up the chauffeur's job six months back."

"Sheikh catch you on the back seat with another of his wives?"

The sidekick laughed; it was more a snicker than a laugh.

Tom said nothing. The club had been Soraya's idea; she had once been the sheikh's favourite belly-dancer. The place was beginning to show a modest profit.

"When will I be flown back?" Tom asked.

"First plane tomorrow."

"What will I get for this?" Tom added. "Life imprisonment?"

Neither CIA man said anything for a while. Then Powers closed the dossier. "That's the normal sentence. But there's an irony about your case, Bradley. You see, all that stuff you and your fancy woman sold was worthless. Pure garbage. Dreamed up by my department."

Powers spoke slowly, relishing every word. The CIA had long suspected a Russian sleeper was operating in Washington. So when they realized Tom was stealing information from Brodie's office, they had allowed it to continue in the hope of smoking the agent out. And it had worked. The only thing they had not expected was for Tom to skip the country.

"Don't *you* find that ironic, Bradley? That the Ruskie was paying good money for trash? And you were the dupe?"

They laughed.

Tom tried to join in, but his lips felt frozen. He was on the receiving end of the much-talked about dirty-tricks department. No wonder all those confidential files had been left lying around Mr Brodie's office! They had been an *invitation*.

"But that doesn't let *you* off the hook, Bradley," Powers went on, watching the overhead fan carve into a smoke ring. "Oh no, pal. *You* didn't know the stuff you were selling wasn't your government's secrets. So you're going to be charged as a Grade One Spy, Bradley. And that will certainly mean life."

Once again Tom sat, stony-faced, as the CIA men chuckled.

Powers became expansive. "Make it easier on yourself, Bradley. The CIA has influence. Make a full confession, now, and we'll do everything we can to help. Do you read me?"

Perfectly, Tom thought. It was a crude attempt at plea bargaining. And did he detect a note of desperation in Powers' voice?

"That NATO file was printed on specially treated paper, Bradley. Every one of its pages has a full set of finger- and thumb-prints of your left hand.

"We simply compare *your* prints with those on the file . . . and you're sunk. The judge will almost certainly hand out the maximum sentence . . ."

As Powers' voice went on, turning the screw tighter, Tom's thoughts flew back. He had worn his chauffeur's gloves at the library's photocopier. But he had taken off his left glove to be able to turn over the pages more quickly.

As evidence in court, it would be damning; but it didn't matter now. These two CIA hatchet-men didn't know it, yet, but he was going to walk out of the room a free man.

"You haven't got a case against me." He spoke softly, but firmly. *"You can't compare my prints."*

"Is this your idea of a joke, Bradley?" Powers said.

Tom smiled grimly. "You could say that. And the joke's on both of us."

He raised his left hand, slowly, and placed it on the desk-top. The fingers and thumb had an unnatural smoothness.

The next morning, as Soraya lay sleeping, Tom watched the dawn break from their balcony. He watched the sun peak above minarets and terracotta roof-tops, framed by the huge dome of the mosque. Soon the bell would sound the call for Islamic prayer. The town would come alive. A new day would begin.

Tom faced himself honestly. He had not been happy about selling his country's secrets—but he was weak. He had never been able to resist the temptation of easy money. It made it easier to live with his conscience, now, knowing that he had not really passed on anything useful to the Soviet agent. And there was a curious irony in that he had helped—albeit unknowingly—the CIA to nail the man.

Overhead, Tom heard the whine of jet engines as they hauled their payload into the crystal-clear dawn sky. The London plane. The two CIA men would be on it, on the first leg of their trip back to the States.

He smiled. Would he ever forget the looks on their faces when he had explained why he had to give up his job as a chauffeur?

There had been a charity ball, six months earlier, organized by the wives of the local oil tycoons. He had never seen so much jewellery on display in any one place before. It had stirred up all his old criminal instincts. Besides, jewellery was easy to transport and no problem to fence.

But the months of soft living with Soraya had dulled his reflexes. He had allowed himself to get caught with a pocketful of diamond necklaces.

Tom had discovered that Islamic law did not discriminate in favour of foreigners; that it dealt harshly with thieves. Very harshly.

He stared at the appendage strapped on to the end of his left forearm. He had hated the sight of the thing at first; now, he was beginning to think of it as a part of himself.

His physiotherapist would be arriving soon, with a new set of exercises. The physiotherapist thought Tom might soon be able to drive a car again.

Of course, he reflected, it would never have the same dexterity as a real hand. But it was a thousand times better than no hand at all.

EXIT LINE

Reginald Hill

THERE IS A chair.

There is a table.

There is an iron bedstead.

There is a bucket.

There is no window.

The walls, ceiling and floor are of the same untreated concrete. Only gravity distinguishes them. Even the door does not help much. It is flush with the wall like the door of a squash court and it is set in the centre of the wall about four feet from the ground and equidistant from the ceiling.

The only light in the room comes from a single bulb set above the door. It is protected by a metal muzzle. There is no switch. It goes out when I get into bed and comes on when I get up.

The door is made of some very hard wood. There is no handle or keyhole and it fits so snugly into the wall that no crack remains wide enough to admit even a sheet of paper.

I sleep wrapped in a square grey blanket on the metal mesh of the bedstead. The temperature of the room never varies. I would put it around sixty-five Fahrenheit.

Hunger, fatigue and the movement of my bowels are my only clock.

There are a few inches of chemical solution in the bucket, but despite this the room must smell abominably. Fortunately I cannot tell.

My bucket is emptied and my rations supplied while I sleep. My rations consist of a soft plastic jug of water, a cob loaf, a lump of cheese, two apples and a bone with a few scraps of meat on it.

I try to stay awake as long as possible after going to bed, but always sleep comes and I have neither seen nor heard any sign of those who clean out my bucket and bring my food.

I exercise each day, following a routine of press-ups, stretches, running on the spot and deep breathing. I think I am still fairly fit despite everything they have done to me, but I have no mirror to check my appearance.

I cannot work out why the door is in the middle of the wall. Perhaps there was once a flight of steps leading up to it. I can find no trace of them, however.

There is always paper on the table and newly sharpened pencils. I have to write every day. If I do not write, I get no food, only water.

The door is made of very hard wood and has no handle or keyhole. If I am to get out of here I must find some means of opening it.

I have to write the story of my life. Each morning I look to see if what I wrote the previous day has gone. If it is still there, then I know I must rewrite it. Sometimes I have done the same episode a dozen times before it is accepted. Sometimes the alteration of a single word is enough.

These notes are the framework of my sanity.

My clothes consist of a pair of blue denim trousers with zipped flies and no belt, a loose shirt, or rather smock, of grey cotton, a pair of open sandals without buckles or laces. I also have a wristwatch on a canvas strap. The face is cracked and it does not work. Hunger, fatigue and the movement of my bowels are my only clock.

Sometimes I think that the walls of the room are getting closer together. I have measured the breadth and width of the room with my feet, placing one in front of the other from corner to corner. It is fifteen foot-lengths square. I do this measurement at least once every day. I know it will not change, but I cannot sit writing for any length of time without doing the measurement.

I have tried banging on the door with my chair but no one comes and the door shows no sign of damage. It sounds so solid that perhaps no noise is audible outside. Not that that matters. I do not doubt I am watched all the time.

I have developed a habit of doodling and scribbling on sheets of paper. Then sometimes I tear and fold these sheets to make aeroplanes, dancing men, flowers or cockleshell boats. But always I contrive to secrete that one of the torn scraps which has my note on it. I dare not write more but I need what I write. These notes are the framework of my sanity.

Any hope I have lies in that door. I laid a trap, putting my toilet bucket directly beneath it. It wasn't much of a trap and absolutely worthless if I am being watched. I tried to lie awake but eventually fell asleep. The bucket was emptied and back in its usual place when I woke.

I suspect I am being injected with drugs as I sleep. I have noticed tiny punctures appearing in my skin and I can think of no other explanation. Perhaps they are trying to make me dependent on some drug so that withdrawal will force me to talk. About what?

I must make contact. Only through contact can there be a future for me.

I need these notes to keep some check on the present. Without them I would not know if things change. I keep them concealed beneath my smock. My broken watch has a luminescent dial. By this tiny light I read my notes under the blanket before I fall to sleep. Without them I think I should be mad. Even with them, I have no certainty of survival. Above all I fear those punctures in my skin. I must force them to show themselves.

Yesterday I stood on my chair and poured cold water through the protective muzzle on to the light bulb. It cracked and went out. I then stood by the door holding the chair ready to attack anyone who entered. But no one came. The room was in pitch darkness. I waited for what seemed several hours, then I grew so fatigued that I sat on the floor. Eventually I fell asleep. When I awoke the light was on again.

I need these notes to keep some check on the present. I have scarcely any memory of the recent past. My broken watch is stopped at a quarter to four. I cannot recall how it got broken. Perhaps I do not want to. But the more autobiography I write, the more my childhood comes back to me. I write in such detail that I shall be old before I reach my youth. Yet whenever I omit anything the writing is not accepted.

My fears that the room is contracting are with me always. I must make contact. I shall refuse to write until they contact me or I starve.

I have written nothing for three days. On the third day I woke up very weak from lack of food and found I was lying on the ceiling of the room. Up above, or down below, I could see the chair, the table, the bucket and the bed. I tried to crawl down the walls to them but I stuck to the ceiling like a fly. Finally I either fainted or fell asleep. When I awoke I was in my bed again and there was food on the table. I ate and started writing immediately.

The door is set in the centre of the wall. There is no crack big enough to admit even a razor blade. It is so solid that it cannot be broken down. Perhaps it will burn. I have an idea for starting a fire. But I have had ideas for so many things.

I have been trying to write of the death of my mother for the past three? four days? Each time what I write is rejected. Why? What do they want of me? I shall write no more.

I have to write again. More and more I think of death but it must be quick. I have no will to die of starvation. My attempt to start a fire was a fiasco. I cleared everything from my table, picked a few small splinters of wood from the surface with my fingernails, then held a pencil between both my palms and rubbed violently, trying to generate heat where the pencil point touched the woodwork. It got warm but nothing more.

I have written that I was not wholly sorry at my mother's death. This is a lie but they have accepted it. They have accepted a lie. How many other lies have they made me tell? I must make an end to this while I still can.

I have decided to hang myself. There is no other way. I thought of slashing my wrists as I lay under my blanket one night, but I have nothing to use. I tried to break my water jug but it just bounces. If I had the courage I could bite through the veins but even in my despair that thought revolts me. But I shall use my teeth to cut through the bound edge of my blanket so that I can tear off a strip to make a noose.

The only light in the room comes from a single bulb set above the door. It is protected by a metal muzzle fitted into the wall. This must be my gallows. The thought frightens me more than I can say, but I see no alternative. I write lies all the time now, descriptions of childhood hatreds and deceptions and odious lusts and imaginings, all lies, all lies. Yet they are accepted, every one of them.

I have my noose. I wish it had not to be this way. How much better to slash my wrists as I lie on my bed and feel the life pour softly from me.

I keep my noose around my waist. All is ready. I climbed on my chair today and examined the light. Let them think what they will.

I had to make sure I had the right length of "rope". No point in ending up on tiptoe slowly strangling. Oh God! But I will strangle. The drop cannot be deep enough to break my neck.

Perhaps they will come if they see me strangling. Perhaps my piece of blanket will break or stretch and leave me flat-footed on the ground. If only I could be certain. Sometimes in the past I have had in my rations a flat brittle shoulder-bone. If I had one of these now I could break a splinter off and stab myself with it or slash my wrists. I must have certainty. I cannot face being hauled back from the brink.

More lies today. And another knuckle-bone. I cannot go on much longer.

Oh God! Today a shoulder! They will wonder at my appetite to see me gnawing and cracking at it. I have a long thin splinter, surprisingly strong but with a point like a needle. I feel as joyous as if someone had given me freedom.

Was it yesterday I was so joyful? Yet I am still here. A noose round my waist, a dagger of bone at my side, yet I am still here. Is it illusion that I think I remember a time when I had will and courage and conviction? If there was a button on the table before me which I merely had to press to obliterate all this place and me with it, could I reach out my finger and press it? Perhaps I have arrived where they want me to arrive. Perhaps now all I have to do is wait.

My dear friends, for what else should I call those who have watched over me with such unstinting care all these weeks? months? years?—my dear friends, these are the last words I shall write in this stinking cell. Yesterday you saw me sitting like a zombie staring blindly into space. Today you will be interested to observe this sudden last outburst of creative energy. And when it is finished you shall at last see me make my suicide attempt. All will be as you have doubtless forecast. Why should it not be, for you must be clever men? But you must not retain to yourself sole claim on the power of prognostication. We on our side have been trained also. And whose school is the better?

I laid my plans within a couple of days—so far as I can gauge—of arriving here. I knew I had to. It's all a question of taking the initiative. Sit and wait, and very soon you are totally under control. This business of autobiography is very seductive. By the time I came to the politically significant period in my life I've no doubt I would have been providing you with dense detail just to convince you of my accuracy! So against your routine I had to set a counter-routine. But *I* am not so stupid as to imagine *you* are so stupid as not to look for this. So I worked out a double routine, the top layer of which you could penetrate easily enough. All those little notes of mine with their hints of breakdown, their wild hopes, their repetitions, did you imagine I would not guess that you would read them? More! I have lain there and felt your hands remove them from under my smock, then replace them after they'd been copied. That surprises you? There is much to surprise you!

I let all my hopes for escaping from here seem to centre on the door. But within a very short while I'd worked out that the door was a dummy. A little piece of hair stuck across the wood and the wall confirmed that it never opened or shut. I then set about discovering the real door. My exercises enabled me to examine most of the floor area without being too obvious and my "shrinking cell" fears allowed me to pace slowly right into the corners and stand there, as if making sure that the walls weren't moving. Really, of course, what I wanted to discover was that the walls did move! But your interior decorator is pretty good and it took another hair in the corner to convince me that the section of wall behind my bed must slide or swing open.

The next thing was to confirm this. I'd worked out that I was certainly being drugged to put me to sleep so soundly that your visits did not disturb me. This meant the food or the water had been tampered with, probably both. Not to eat would draw too much attention, I thought, but you co-operated to the extent of withdrawing my food if I did not write. So I deliberately did not write one day and this just left me with the problem of the water. I had noticed the calibrations on the inside of the jug and I knew it was not merely enough to pretend to drink—this was not just a one-off thing. I would need to repeat it at least once, probably twice, till all my theories were checked. So I decided to kill two birds with one stone and see if I could put the light out of action.

It worked beautifully. When the cold water cracked the hot bulb I crouched in the darkness as though waiting to attack the first man through that dummy door. Gradually, as you would expect having seen me apparently drink quite a lot of water before my experiment, I pretended to grow drowsy. Finally I flopped over as if asleep. I could have embraced the man who came through the wall and picked me up, even when he stuck a pin in me to check the depth of my sleep! Fortunately I had already worked out what this rash of punctures meant and I was ready for it. I hope my fears of being turned into a junkie entertained you. Fear and the human imagination are all the drugs the expert interrogator needs.

Now I needed to do this once more to establish the routine. I hope I kept you amused with my attempts to break down the door and set fire to it! How natural that at last full of despair I should turn to thoughts of suicide. And how equally natural, I hope, that in my search for a weapon I should attempt to shatter my jug and thus spill all the water again—on a day, of course, when I was foodless for being naughty.

Again I had to go through the motions of drowsiness and finally sleep. I hope I got the timing right, but as this must be uncertain in any case as it's related to the amount of water I drink, perhaps it didn't matter. But it mattered thereafter.

Counting seconds, I reached eighty minutes before the wall slid open. I have had to take what happened then as the routine sequence for I do not dare risk another trial run.

The light went on as the wall slid open (I'm writing this for my benefit, dear friends, not yours!), a single figure entered, stuck a pin into me as before. Ready though I was I twitched slightly and he tried again. This time I showed no reaction and this satisfied him. That must be some drug you're using!

His job seemed to be pretty menial so far as I could make it out. He simply removed the jug and the toilet bucket. As he left, another two men arrived. They removed my notes from their hiding-place and photographed the latest one before returning them. Then they photographed what I had written during the day.

(The original I found on the table still when I got up, so clearly rejection has nothing to do with content. It is merely aimed at setting up doubts and anxieties in the writer so that the search for detail is pursued with great vigour each time. *What* clever men you must be!)

I knew that these two were not you, my dear friends, for they talked like underlings. Not indiscreetly, of course, for they, too, would be on your video screen, but of ordinary things like the foulness of the weather and the approach of Christmas.

As they finished, the first man (I assume) returned with my bucket and my next day's rations. I had written that day, so my food was restored.

Now I had all the information I needed or at least was likely to get to enable me to escape. So now the plan could really get under way.

I wrote more and more of suicide. I made a noose. I was interested to observe that although you knew I had a noose, you didn't take it off me. So I wondered if you could be provoked into giving me a weapon, that is the bone dagger.

I bet this caused some debate between the two of you. Yes, I've come to the conclusion that there are probably two of you sitting up there like gods watching my behaviour on a flickering grey screen. One of you will be a military man, concerned with security, duty, following orders, protecting the state. He wouldn't be very happy at the thought of my having anything which could be called a weapon.

The other must be a scientist, fascinated by the opportunity to acquire new knowledge and to test old. This is no weapon, but a token, he would say. The prisoner has no real intention of committing suicide. To give the possibility of death is to give the hope of life and it is from this that true confessions will spring. Besides what if I did die? Even failed experiments are useful. The unexpected becomes expected once it has happened.

So I got my weapon. A bonus of bone! See, I can still make jokes, scientist. What does that prove of the human spirit? But it really was a bonus. The main function of my suicide pretensions has been to permit me to play around with the light again. You've seen me examine it, ostensibly as a hook to hang myself on. Shortly you shall see me get back up there once again, and I doubt if you'll be surprised. I must look as if I'm building up to some climax of action, which indeed I am. Yesterday I sat as if in a coma, staring into space. Today I have been scribbling in an agitated fashion. I bet you can hardly wait to see what I've been writing, scientist!

Very shortly I shall jump up and begin to pace around the room looking as if I'm breaking up. Then suddenly I will push the chair under the light. Next I shall unwind my noose of blanket from my waist and examine it as though both fascinated and horrified. I shall put my hand to my throat, have a bout of coughing as though the very *thought* of hanging restricts my breathing. (I bet you make a note of that!) Picking up my jug, I shall take a draught of water to stop the coughing. And finally I shall climb on the chair and loop the noose over the light fitment.

This is the big moment. The soldier may want to interfere (they can be very humane, soldiers. They like to kill to timetables). The scientist will say *wait*. The struggle will show itself in every angle of my body.

And life will win. I will relax, sob convulsively, almost be sick. The scientist will preen himself.

And I shall be squirting the water held in my mouth into the little cockleshell of paper I have tied into the noose. The keel of this paper boat, of a kind you've grown very used to seeing over the past few weeks, has a tiny hole in it. As I clamber off the chair, the water will already begin to seep through. I shall look exhausted. Who wouldn't be in my circumstances, drained of emotion and topped up with drugged water?

I shall stagger across the room and fall on the bed. The light will go out. (Is it economy or convention that makes you switch off when I go to bed?) And a moment or so later, if all goes well and the fates who have so maligned me these past months decide to wink, while the bulb is still red hot the water will drip through and crack the glass and you up aloft in your godlike observation post will not be aware of it.

So in one hour and twenty minutes (if he is as punctilious as my military friend must surely require) the man with the pin will open the door. Only this time no light will go on and I shall be waiting with my pin also.

After that, who knows? If once I get outside, I'm sure that I shall find myself in remote enough terrain to make escape possible. The way my photographer friends talked about the rough winds and snow on the hills gives me a picture of a countryside with plenty of undulations to hide in, lots of flowing water to shake off dogs, lots of trees (pine forests, perhaps?) to ward off helicopters.

We shall see. You, my friends, I should have liked to meet. But I shall not be able to arrange it, I fear. If I escape, distance—and if I don't, death—will separate us beyond hope of encounter. Either way, you my soldier with all your schemes of security, and you my scientist with all your charts of the human mind, you both will have been defeated. You deserve death also, but perhaps defeat will serve as well for your puffed-up egos. Let the curtain rise!

"The thing about the human mind," said the scientist with great satisfaction, "is that even its deceits are forecastable. A lie is as good as the truth to the discerning eye."

"If you were so sure 128 was going, I wouldn't have a man in hospital with a punctured lung," growled the soldier.

"I'm sorry about that," said the scientist. "But I had to let things run their course. All those notes! What ingenuity. I look forward to observing the reaction to recapture."

"If there is a recapture," said the soldier.

"What on earth do you mean? You assured me security was complete!" said the scientist.

"It is," said the soldier. "Look at the map on the screen. That bleep and flashing light comes from the bugs. Every item of 128's clothing has got one attached. Lose a sandal, it makes no difference. My men can track every movement. Only . . ."

"Only what?"

"Only there's nothing but your fancy theories to say that it won't be a corpse they bring back!"

"I've told you," said the scientist. "128's not suicidal. All this talk of death or escape is self-deceit. That light seems to be following the line of the stream, doesn't it?"

"Yes. The usual pattern. We could have worked it out even without the bugs. The letter told us, though we hardly needed that either. A valley for concealment, running water to throw the dogs off the scent. Dogs! They must think we live in the dark ages."

"The light's moving pretty fast."

"It's a fast-moving stream."

"You don't mean 128's actually in the water?" said the scientist, suddenly alarmed.

"Why not? Swimming, floating, it's the fastest way down to the sea."

"Let's have a look at the file," said the scientist. "Nothing here about being a strong swimmer."

"You don't have to be," said the soldier with grim satisfaction. "Dead or alive, that water'll move you fast. Don't look so worried! There's a net across the mouth of the stream and my men are waiting there."

"I hope so. I hope so," said the scientist. "But nets are more holes than string."

"There's no way through. And even if there were, no one's going to stay alive for long in the Irish Sea on a winter's day. Poor sod. The things I do for England. Look, there you are! Like I said, in the net."

The light had halted where the line of the stream intersected the line of the shore.

A telephone rang.

"Back in the fold," said the soldier, picking it up.

He listened for a few moments and then said, "Good God!"

"What's up?" demanded the scientist. "Not dead?"

"No," said the soldier. "All they found was a bundle of clothes tied to a log."

"Maximum security screen!" he barked into the mouthpiece. "Then start searching. I'm coming down."

He replaced the receiver.

"Maximum security?" sneered the scientist.

The soldier paused at the door.

"Has it struck you yet that the letter was probably just as big a smoke-screen as the notes?" he asked coldly. "So much for psychology."

"Rubbish," said the scientist, peering into the thick file before him. "No one's that controlled. Show 'em freedom or vengeance, every time they'll run."

The soldier said nothing but gave a little gasp and stepped back a pace from the open doorway.

The scientist looked up from the file.

"You OK?" he asked.

The soldier turned. His hands clutched his belly. About his tight-laced fingers was coiled a thread of blood.

"Psychology!" he whispered scornfully.

Then he fell.

Behind him in the doorway stood a naked woman. She stepped into the room.

In her hand was a dagger of bone.

BE LUCKY*

Allan Prior

LUCKY SAT IN the darkened room over the little bistro on the Boulevard Hélène and waited for the stitches to be taken out. This had been the hardest part of all, the waiting. Almost two weeks of it. It seemed more like two years.

Lucky could not sleep properly for he could not lie down in case the stitches pulled and split and had to be sewn back into his inflamed face once more. So he dozed upright on the hard chair and suffered. It had been ten days since the German doctor had put them in, working silently with scalpel and needle. Only once had he spoken. "You may not be quite so handsome, later. Do you mind that?"

Lucky had not replied. Handsome! It was the word everybody had always used about him. The handsomest man in the room, in the regiment, in the casino.

Lucky would have grimaced if he could. Where had handsome got him except this dirty little room, his face and his hair-line cut and clipped at by a man he couldn't see and whose name he didn't know? What did his face look like now? Something in a butcher's shop, he supposed.

Well, he thought grimly, he could live without his looks. In a way they had dictated all his actions. A man who looked as he did had to act as he did. Had to gamble as he did, raise hell as he did. Top stakes every time, let it ride and the hell with it. That had been his style, nobody could deny it.

*The disappearance of Lord Lucan in the wake of a famous murder has led to endless speculation. On the seventh anniversary of his disappearance, this short story by Allan Prior, writer of television's *Z Cars, Softly, Softly* and *The Sweeney*, appeared in the London *Daily Mail*. It was written as pure fiction, but . . . ?

Now, the doctor had said, he would have to change all that. He would have to be cautious. Anyway, until he got there, until he was under the General's protection. The General was looking forward to meeting him. If he did exactly as he was told and the luck ran his way, he had nothing to worry about.

Luck? He had lived with it, on it, by it, all his life.

"Be lucky, guv," the taxi-driver had said as he dropped him at Victoria, the night it all started; automatic cockney matiness, that was all, but Lucky had only just stopped himself over-tipping the man (that might be remembered) and had contented himself with a gruff, "We all need that."

Alone, on Victoria Station forecourt with some damfool idea of getting a boat-train, he must have been mad. Every port, every airport would be watched by now surely? Well, his luck had held. Nobody had noticed the tall lone figure. Not even in the public telephone-box, as his head clearing a little from the frightful events of the night, he called the one man of all his friends he knew he could rely on. This friend knew everybody and everything. He was another who played for high stakes. Another who understood. His friend had been in, lucky again; his voice had been cool, he had hardly sounded surprised. He had asked, "Where's the car?" and when Lucky had told him he had said, "I'll take care of that." He had cut short Lucky's ramblings with a curt, "Never mind that, old boy, the thing is to get you out."

Out?

Lucky shifted on the hard chair in the darkened room over the bistro. His fingers brushed his bare upper lip where the thick guardee's moustache had been. Out? The hours after Victoria had been blurred. The dark limo that picked him up outside the coffee bar, and his friend's arm around him in the leathery interior, the flask of brandy at his lips. All that was still vivid. Even his friend's warning. "I've taken the best advice. And that's a boat. We're driving to the East Coast now, staying over one night at a cottage I know. You'll go tomorrow night. Good job you've got your overcoat, you'll be needing it."

At the sand-dunes his friend had said goodbye, probably, Lucky supposed, for the last time. It was dark and wild that night and the sea boiled behind them. "I have to get back, old boy, they'll be asking me questions, I have no doubt." His friend's voice dropped. "These people can be trusted. I've paid them and there's more when they get you there. Do as they say, they're professionals, usually they smuggle dope." He held both of Lucky's hands a long, long moment. "Be lucky," said his friend, and turned back towards his limo parked on the lonely road beyond the sand-dunes.

Lucky watched him until he was out of sight and turned to the three silent foreign-looking men in jeans and sailor caps. They gestured to a rowing boat on the beach. "Hope you're a good sailor, sir," said one, smiling.

Lucky nodded but did not reply, and walked calmly towards the boat. Out at sea, beyond the shallows, he could see the dark shape of a motor yacht, bobbing in the surf. He got in and the men rowed. Once on the yacht—and it had been a grabbing, slippery business getting aboard—he was given a glass of rum. He drank it and the man offered him another. "I am all right," Lucky said. "Put it away."

The French coast had been grey and grim in the dawn light. There had been a car waiting. He had waited in this room ever since. That had been (he did the sum again in his head) twelve days ago, no fourteen, he had forgotten the two days he had sat alone before the doctor appeared. There had been food and drink in the room but the door had been locked. In the next room he could hear a tart plying her trade.

There were shutters across the windows and a note from his friend on the table. The message had been brief. *Do exactly as they say. Take care. Good luck.* There had also been £1,000 in mixed currencies, French, German, Brazilian, Paraguayan. Lucky had stared at those notes for a long time, and at last he thought he understood. He had burned his friend's note in a saucer and smoked the packet of Gaulois left on the table. The wine he had sipped, the food he left untouched. He had tried not to think.

He had not succeeded.

The German doctor (Lucky supposed he was German, possibly Austrian, did it matter?) had been businesslike but not talkative. He said the news was good, the car had been found, the news-papers mostly thought he was dead. That had been four days ago.

Today, the stitches came out.

At last the key in the door turned and the doctor slipped in. He was prim and shaven, darkly dressed and, Lucky guessed, sixty. Lucky somehow knew he was a man who had done this many times before, a man whose profession it was. "Good morning," said the doctor and Lucky asked, "Have a drink?" and the doctor said, "Not until I have finished." He took off his gloves and opened his case and laid out his instruments on the table, and shone the portable pencil-light on Lucky's face and took the bandages from Lucky's eyes and mouth very, very slowly, hissing softly as he did so. He took the stitches out very, very gently, and at last he stood back.

"So," he said. "Very good. Yes. I think so."

Lucky said nothing. He felt nothing except a sudden deep tiredness.

"Don't you want to see your new self?" asked the doctor, softly.

"I suppose so." In truth he did not. He liked himself as he was. But that, he supposed, was all over. He nodded, and the doctor, keeping the pencil-light on him, held up the small sharp mirror.

Lucky stared at the face. It was somebody else, somebody vaguely familiar. But not himself, not Lucky. Never in a million years.

The doctor seemed to be waiting for something, so Lucky said, "Damn good, I must say."

Even his voice seemed different.

He sat in the room another week, quite alone, the tart popping his day's supply of food in each morning, not looking at him, until the doctor came again and examined his face, which had almost healed. "We'll put some powder on," said the doctor, "after I have cut your hair and so on."

So Lucky's hair was now short and dyed grey and he was ten pounds lighter. Looking at himself in the mirror, Lucky was shocked. It all seemed unreal. The doctor brought him a suit, nothing like the kind of suit he was used to, the sort of suit he never expected to wear. For one thing, somebody else had worn it and it smelled of tobacco and stale sweat. The doctor grimaced. "It is not for long. Now there is only the photograph." A man appeared behind him, snapped a shutter and left. Lucky did not even see his face. The photograph, when it came, attached to the strange-looking passport, looked like that of somebody else, somebody old and possibly ill, somebody who had never been rich.

The car ride to the airport scared Lucky, whom nothing had ever scared before. God dammit, he thought, shaking. I'd be better off back *there*, facing it out. This isn't me. It's somebody else, shaking and sweating in this rotten old suit. He stared through his steel-rimmed spectacles with the plain glass, and swallowed. Steady. The doctor's hand pressed his arm. "Nothing to worry about. Soon we'll be on the plane. The odds are on our side."

"You're coming with me?"

Lucky was astonished at the gratitude in his voice.

"But of course, my dear fellow, you're my patient."

My God, his legs had turned to jelly as he stumbled towards the desk and the doctor had explained, "My friend is not too well but he's looking forward to his trip on the big bird," and they had been all smiles at the desk as he had recovered (the bored security man did not even look his way) and nodded apologetically ("Don't speak, ever," the doctor had warned him), and then he was on Concorde and despite his terror he had looked curiously around him. But the doctor had given him a pill, and he had slept, dreamlessly. I've slept my way to freedom, he thought, waking to see the Christ-figure on the mountain-top, far below, and the blue water and the long strip of golden sand.

Rio was a town he would once have taken delight in, have caroused and gambled wildly in, but his place in Rio was another small room in a small dingy hotel, while his passage further west was arranged. "Too many bounty hunters in Rio," said the doctor. "Once you are under the General's protection you will be safe."

And now he was here. The series of fast cars had at last turned into a military jeep, there had been a bridge, a river, a crossing of a frontier, a lot of laughter from the soldiers who drove and guarded the jeep. Then he was in a villa of some sort with the German doctor still at his elbow, smiling now. A door opened to a brightly lit room and, blinking at the light, he saw across the splendid table a middle-aged Germanic-looking man whom he instantly recognized, or anyway he knew who it must be: the General; and Lucky knew that he was safe here, along with the concentration-camp murderers and the Gestapo men and anybody else who could pay the price and seemed the right sort.

Lucky also knew that nobody who came to this place ever left it. There was nowhere to go from here, except back to the avengers.

The General extended a meaty hand, smiling. "My dear fellow, we have waited up to welcome you. We were beginning to wonder if your famous luck had run out."

Lucky smiled back and took his hand.

"Not yet," he said, knowing in his heart that it had.

THE OLD HADDOCK

H. R. F. Keating

THERE WAS NO pleasing the Old Haddock, thought Sergeant Prowdon as he sent the big Daimler pushing fast—or as fast as one travelled in the 1930s—through the quiet summer night of the deserted Kentish lanes.

All right, so they had to get the old fogey out of his bed. But he was meant to be a policeman same as anybody else, even if he should have been retired long ago.

Sitting forward half an inch more over the wheel, the sergeant pushed up their speed another three miles an hour.

At least it should not take long to get there.

"Well," he said aloud, "we'll be on the scene in five minutes now, Inspector."

The Old Haddock sat there beside him hunched in his dark overcoat—an overcoat in midsummer, would you believe it!—and with his invariable bowler hat tilted forward over his eyes. And he said not a word.

Sergeant Prowdon concentrated on the hedge-shrouded road ahead.

If the Old Haddock didn't want to talk to him, then the sergeant could stay silent with the best of them.

And at once the old boy spoke. "Tottenham," he said. "Refresh my memory, Sergeant. I must be getting old."

Prowdon blinked. "Don't quite get you, Inspector."

"Get you," the Old Haddock snorted. "What sort of expression is that? An Americanism, I suppose."

"Land of progress, sir," Prowdon said, determined not to give in to the old idiot on everything.

"Progress," came a snort from his side. "I see they're putting on stage shows now about the family of that Chicago gangster they shot some time ago. Well, that's not the sort of progress we want in good old England, thank you very much."

"No, Inspector."

The Old Haddock.

"And I asked you a question, Sergeant."

Prowdon braked sharply as the gates of a big house showed up in the Daimler's headlights.

"Sorry, sir. Can't quite—"

"I asked what you knew about Mr Miles Tottenham, Sergeant. The man whose house you're driving us to at this ridiculous speed."

Prowdon bit back the expletive that rose to his lips.

"Mr Tottenham," he said, "he's the famous explorer, sir. There's bits about him in the *Kentish Times* every now and again."

"Yes, Sergeant, I am well aware that Mr Tottenham is a famous explorer. But there's something else about him I can't quite lay my tongue to. Something not entirely to his credit."

"That would be his mutiny, sir," Prowdon said, pleased with himself for being able to recall details that had defeated the Old Haddock.

"Yes," he continued, as more big houses began to show up one by one in the leafy darkness on either side. "Yes, he was out all on his own in the Amazon or somewhere, and his bearers—if that's what the poor bloody devils are called—wanted to turn back. So he started shooting 'em one by one. Shot hundreds before he got his way, so they say."

"Not hundreds, Sergeant."

Prowdon darted the Old Haddock a glance of fury.

"Thought you couldn't recollect the circumstances, sir."

"No more I can, Sergeant. But I've still got a bit of brain in my head. If Mr Tottenham had hundreds of natives with him he wouldn't have just been exploring; he'd have been a general in charge of an Expeditionary Force. And we've never conquered South America yet."

"It was just a figure of speech, sir," Prowdon explained.

"Exactly, Sergeant."

The Old Haddock.

Then on the grass bank, beside a big pair of open gates, the sergeant spotted a narrow board with the words "Fair Acres" painted on it.

"This'll be it then, sir," he said. "Sir Ellis What's-his-name should be waiting for us somewhere."

"Sir Ellis Sturge, Sergeant."

The Old Haddock straightened his bowler.

Going to go all "family retainer" on us, I suppose, Prowdon thought. Just because the fellow's been Governor of some colony or other. And off any day to exploit another one, too.

He turned the big car in at the gates and advanced along the drive, the headlights showing up plentiful signs of the comfortable life—the gravel ahead immaculately weed-free, the big flower border with every clump of plants well staked and tied, the discreet outhouse, now the gardeners' toolshed no doubt, to judge by the spade plunged in the ground by its padlocked door.

"Now just tell me once again exactly what that message was," the Old Haddock said, with heavy emphasis on the "exactly".

"Give it to you word for word if you want, Inspector."

"I do want."

Prowdon brought the car to a halt, revved up the engine, and switched off. He sat up to attention in the darkness and recited.

"Message received by telephone at one twenty-two a.m. Caller's name: Sir Ellis Sturge. Message ran: 'You the CID? Good. Then you'd better get round here pretty quickly. I've just found a body. Dead. Head knocked in with a bloody shovel, right in the middle of the lawn. Place called The Laurels—god-awful name. But you'd better report to the house next door. Fair Acres, Mr Miles Tottenham. That's where I'm phoning from. Got that? Good. Then at the double, if you please.' End of message."

In the middle of the dark mass in front of them that was the house a sudden oblong of yellow light appeared as the big front door abruptly swung open.

A figure came out and strode toward them. He was a man of exceptional height, a good six foot three, and he held himself with the erectness that only long training can achieve. It was difficult to make out the man's features but the white hair of his bare head stood out clearly in the light of a cloud-hidden moon.

"You the police wallahs?"

Sergeant Prowdon winced at the exaggeratedly drawling tone of the voice—that arrogantly bland voice-of-command that had once ruled a world-straddling empire.

But the Old Haddock slipped out of the car and ran round to the front at a respectful crouch, his rapidly removed bowler held crown outward in front of him.

"Inspector Hadley from the Chislehurst CID, sir," he said. "Am I addressing Sir Ellis Sturge?"

"Certainly you are. I sent for you, didn't I? And now you are here, you'd better listen pretty hard. Can only spare you two minutes. Got to be at Croydon in half an hour."

He extended a large bony fist, twisted his wrist round, and peered at the watch on it.

"Twenty-eight minutes, actually," he said.

"At Croydon, sir, at two o'clock in the morning?"

Even the Old Haddock can't keep up the respectful tone all the time, Prowdon reflected cheerfully.

"Imperial Airways," Sir Ellis said loftily. "Got to catch one of their planes. Taking up my term of office in Umpala."

"Oh, yes, of course, Sir Ellis."

The Old Haddock gave a little jab of a bow over the clasped bowler.

"Where's your notebook then?" Sir Ellis demanded.

And the Old Haddock actually turned sharply round and barked, "Notebook, Sergeant, notebook."

Prowdon pulled the notebook from his pocket, flipped it open, and stood waiting. As if in answer to an unspoken order from Sir Ellis, a full and golden summer moon came out from behind a cloud to give him enough light to write by. He licked the tip of his pencil.

"Very well," Sir Ellis said. "I was spending the evening in the furnished house I had rented for my leave next door when my neighbour here, Miles Tottenham, came round and invited me over for a farewell drink. At about a quarter past one I left, intending to get into my car and drive over to Croydon. But I decided to take a last look round outside the house—make sure it didn't look too inviting to a burglar. Certain responsibilities in these things, you know. And when I got round to the back I saw this chappie. Dead, of course. Made sure of that. Spanish, I should say. But a sahib all right. Wearing evening dress. So I came straight back round here and got on to you people."

He shot out his left fist again in the same brusque gesture and regarded his watch.

"Have to leave now," he announced. "Strict about time of arrival at Croydon. Quite right, of course. And it would never do if the aeroplane arrived at Umpala, chiefs all gathered waiting to greet me, tribesmen camping there for days, and I didn't present myself on parade."

He shot a quick glance back at the still-open front door of the big house behind him.

"Tottenham'll tell you anything you want to know," he said. "Show you where to look, et cetera, et cetera. And if there is anything you want from me, Government House, Umpala, will find me. Though of course I mustn't be asked to give evidence."

He put his fine beak-nosed head up into the air and inhaled the scents of the night.

"Good-night to you."

And off he strode out of the open gates. A moment or two later the sound of a car engine being brought briskly to life broke the stillness of the night.

And the Old Haddock had just stood there lapping it up, Prowdon thought. Lets a key witness simply walk out on him just because the feller's a bloody nob.

He watched as his superior officer carefully replaced his well-brushed bowler, and then he offered up a silent prayer that the old fogey was not going to let the explorer trample over him, too.

He followed while the Old Haddock marched up the steps of the house, rang at the bell beside the open front door, and remained punctiliously on the visitors' side of the threshold.

But they did not have long to wait.

Scarcely had the sound of the bell pealed out loudly in the empty hall—there seemed to be nothing but trophies of the chase everywhere in it, tiger and leopard skins, horned heads, diamond-shaped shields made from stretched hides, and crossed pairs of native spears—when they heard the sound of heavy feet on the well-carpeted stairs, and Miles Tottenham, the explorer, appeared.

It could be no one else. He was a man of about fifty, so broad-shouldered as to be almost squat, with a face reddened by a thousand tropic suns, a tuft of ginger moustache on his upper lip, and gingery hair springing up all round a balding head. He wore a jacket, waistcoat, and plus-fours of an aggressive brown check.

"Ha," he said, as soon as he saw his visitors, "you're the police. Sturge gone then?"

"Sir Ellis had to be at Croydon Aerodrome by two o'clock, as I daresay you know, Mr Tottenham," the Old Haddock said, swiftly removing the bowler once again.

"Yes, yes. Damned inconvenient for the poor chap," Tottenham replied. "You'll see he's kept well out of this, won't you?"

"You can count on our discretion, sir," the Old Haddock chipped in, quick as a wink.

You bet, Prowdon thought. You can see this Tottenham fellow's never had anything to do but go off and make life hell for a lot of natives. And no doubt coming back richer each time, too. There are some thieves you'll never get behind bars; murderers, too, come to that. Look at the way he shot all those bearers.

"You'll want to see the body straight off," Tottenham said as he stamped down the outside steps. "Sturge tells me it's some sort of foreigner. Wearing a dinner jacket, too."

He made a curious strangled gurgling sound.

"Heaven knows what he was doing next door in the garden at The Laurels," he added.

"I shouldn't wonder if that becomes plain enough once we find out who he is," the Old Haddock said equably. "Routine inquiries generally bring us our answers in the end."

Miles Tottenham issued a sound which Prowdon decided could only be a snort of pure derision.

"Daresay that's true enough of your quiet English crimes," he trumpeted. "But it would hardly do in the parts of the world I'm more at home in. Question of acting pretty damn quickly there, or getting nowhere. Had some trouble of this sort in New Guinea once. Got every soul in the place out in front of me soon as I saw the body. Went along the lines of 'em. Spotted one black man trembling like a leaf. Grabbed him by the hair of his head. 'Well, what you makum kill for, fella?' Had a confession out of him on the spot."

"Indeed, sir. Most interesting."

Tramping glumly behind the pair of them, Prowdon wondered which one he would like to kick harder.

They turned in at the next-door gates of The Laurels and the explorer led them round to the garden behind. And there on the lawn, plain to see in the moonlight, was the body.

"Daresay I should have mounted guard here," Tottenham said. "Bit awkward really. Didn't want to leave Sturge to cope on his own, not when he'd got to get away and all that. And then I've a young wife at home, too. Never do for her to come down and find me not there. No servants in the place, of course. All sleep out nowadays."

"Well, no harm's been done in any event, sir," the Old Haddock said soothingly. "Murder weapon beside the body by the looks of it."

He knelt on one knee on the silvery grass of the moonlit lawn and looked closely at the weapon which lay about two yards from the sprawled body. It was a long-handled coal shovel of wrought iron, blackleaded, and blood was clearly visible on the blade. It certainly looked heavy enough to have inflicted the considerable injury that the dead man's head had received.

Tottenham stood behind the Old Haddock and peered down at the shovel morosely.

"Here, wait a minute," he said suddenly. "I believe I know where that comes from. It's from The Laurels itself. Seen it dozens of times with my own eyes. Saw it tonight, come to that, when I called for Sturge."

The Old Haddock glanced quickly at the big darkened house.

"Sergeant," he said, "take a quick look–see, would you? Any sign of forcible entry. You know what to keep an eye open for."

Prowdon headed for the house, taking care not to hurry himself.

If the murder weapon came from the house which Sir Ellis Sturge had lived in, he reasoned, then it was plain as could be that Sir Ellis should never have been permitted to drive away like that without so much as a by-your-leave. Just because he was going out to govern a lot of natives, it didn't mean he was above committing murder. Especially when the business looked unpremeditated, too, with that great gash in the victim's head and the weapon flung down beside him like that.

Across the lawn in the quiet of the night he heard Miles Tottenham's bark of a voice.

"Good Lord, Inspector, I know the chappie! It's young Mendez, Roberto Mendez. Bit of what you might call a society figure, though bit of a foreigner too. I'd met him at soirées and so forth."

"Had you indeed, sir. Well, that's most helpful, most helpful."

Prowdon stopped in front of a pair of french windows that led from the house out on to the lawn, and then stared at them in sudden interest.

He turned and called across the lawn.

"French windows broken open here, Inspector. Wood all splintered round the lock. Looks as if it might've been done with a spade or something."

The Old Haddock, who was still down on one knee beside the body, rose and was flicking at the dampened blue serge of his stiffly creased trousers in a preoccupied way.

"Just take a quick look inside and see if you can spot the companion pieces to the weapon," he called back. "Don't touch the evidence, mind."

Don't touch the evidence, don't touch the evidence, Prowdon muttered to himself. When does he think I was born?

Gently he opened the french windows with the edge of his pocketknife and then stepped into the room beyond. The moonlight that flooded in from directly behind him showed him what he wanted at first glance. He went across to the fireplace. There, laid neatly on the hearth, was a long poker and a pair of tongs, each in the same design as the coal shovel.

He went back outside to report.

But before he had got across to where the Old Haddock was taking a careful look at the dead man's battered head, kneeling on the other knee this time, a quite unexpected figure burst on the scene.

"Miles. Miles. Miles, what is it? What's happening?"

A young woman had come running into the garden, wearing

nothing more than a blue silk kimono wrapped round her nightdress. She was blonde and boyish, about twenty-five, Prowdon guessed. A somewhat surprising wife for a sandy old devil like Miles Tottenham.

At the sound of her voice the explorer had run towards her. He endeavoured now to interpose his solid stubby frame between her and the body. But vainly, since she was in any case half a head the taller.

"Unfortunate accident," he said in the sort of voice people like him kept for addressing dogs and the less intelligent members of the servant class.

"But what is it, Miles? That man's hurt, isn't he? Is he dead?"

"No, no. Nothing at all for you to worry about, my dear. Now just you let me take you back to bed while the police chappies get on with their job."

"Police? Then it *is* someone dead. He's wearing evening dress, too. Miles, is it someone we know?"

"Now don't you bother your pretty little head with it," the ginger-haired explorer said. "You just come back indoors, and you can make us both some tea or something."

"No."

Her voice rang out sharply in the moon-soaked night.

"June, go back at once!"

But Tottenham's bark had absolutely no effect. His wife broke free from the hand that held her elbow and ran across the lawn towards the body.

Three yards away from it she stopped abruptly.

"Bobby," she said. "It's Bobby. I was right!"

She flung herself down towards the sprawled form.

"Oh, my darling. My darling."

The Old Haddock acted pretty quickly, Prowdon had to hand him that. Before the girl could touch the body he had his arm there, rigidly extended, holding her back.

Her husband came striding up behind her, seized both her elbows, and pulled her to her feet.

"Get back home, you slut," he exploded.

Again she broke from his grasp. But this time she wheeled to face him.

"You," she said tremblingly. "You killed him."

She stared at him, her eyes widening and widening.

"You murderer," she spat. "You bloody murderer. Bobby thought you were going to be away. He must have come in through our back gate, and you saw him. You saw him and you killed him."

Suddenly she launched herself forward, hands up, nails clawing. Prowdon had to run up, grab her, and haul her away with all his strength. He kept a firm hold on her while the explorer wiped away the blood from a long scratch running all the way down his right cheek.

"I'm sorry you think so badly of me, my dear," he said. "But the fact of the matter is, I'm the one person who couldn't have killed that unpleasant young man. We've just this moment established that. He was hit with that coal shovel you see lying there, and that was stolen just before the crime from The Laurels here. Now ever since Sturge left this place I've been in his company. I went and fetched him and I stayed with him all along till just before he found the body. And in any case I wouldn't dirty my hands killing a creature like that. Horsewhip him, yes. I might horsewhip both of you. But he wasn't fit for killing."

Prowdon had to hold the girl even more tightly at this. Afterwards he was to recall the feel of her young struggling body through the thin silks of her kimono and nightdress. But at the time he had no moment to spare for any thoughts except how to make sure she did not wriggle free.

Mercifully the sound of a car drawing up in the road outside came to their ears.

"Ah," said the Old Haddock, "that'll be the police surgeon. I think perhaps we'd all better go back next door."

Once again they walked in a procession. This time the Old Haddock led the way. Prowdon followed keeping an uncompromising grip on Mrs Tottenham's left arm, and the explorer brought up the rear. They stopped when they reached the doctor's car and the Old Haddock explained to him, in what Prowdon thought was an unnecessarily tactful way, that Mrs Tottenham needed attention and that Fair Acres should therefore be his first port of call.

They set off with the doctor. But to Prowdon's surprise the Old Haddock tapped the sergeant on the arm.

"A word with you, my lad," he said.

Prowdon released Mrs Tottenham, who seemed more subdued now. The Old Haddock waited in silence till she had reached the gates of her own house. Then he turned sharply to Prowdon.

"Right, Sergeant," he said. "I want you to get that coal shovel, pick it up so that any possible fingerprints are left intact, put it in the car and drive like hell over to Croydon. I'll get in touch with Imperial Airways on the telephone and try to hold up Sir Ellis's flight. If you get to him in time I want you to show him that shovel. Understand?"

"Show him—but what do I say?"

"Just show it to him. And hurry. You haven't got a moment to lose if he's not to get away."

Standing beside the big aeroplane with its four powerful motors thrumming hard and the great airfield spread out all around in the darkness, Sergeant Prowdon held the coal shovel out to Sir Ellis Sturge.

Sir Ellis took one quick look at it.

"But that isn't the weapon at all," he said irritatedly. "That's one of the fire-irons from that god-awful house I rented. What in heaven's name have you brought me that for?"

And then Prowdon saw it all.

Sir Ellis had found Roberto Mendez, his head knocked in "with a bloody shovel", right in the middle of the lawn. "With a bloody shovel" had been a mere figure of speech. No doubt the weapon had been something more like a spade—like the spade that had been used to force the french windows at The Laurels.

And, of course, that meant that the fiery Miles Tottenham could no longer claim he had not had access to the weapon that killed Mendez. His wife had said that her Bobby had probably come in through the back gate at Fair Acres. Of course he had, and had encountered the hot-tempered explorer who had snatched up a spade, killed Mendez, and then carried the body and weapon to The Laurels garden next door to misdirect the official investigation.

Then later, quick-witted as he was, when he had heard Sir Ellis's exaggerations and figure of speech on the telephone, he had taken extraordinary advantage of them by dodging back to The Laurels, using the murder spade to break in and get hold of the alibi-providing shovel, pressing the shovel into the wound before throwing it down beside the body, and finally, yes, taking the telltale spade back with him and simply plunging it into the cleansing earth right outside his own toolshed.

Fantastically quick and clever, he'd been.

And, damn it all, the Old Haddock had seen through everything. No, not "the old Haddock". More like "the cunning old devil". Call a spade a spade.

THE CALL OF THE RUNNING TIDE

Judy Chard

WHAT WAS LEFT of the submarine was inaccessible at high tide, wedged in the reef of rocks which stretched round the mouth of the cove. The conning tower and part of the deck stood stark against the skyline as the sea receded, rough with barnacles, green with weed, which was crisp and brittle beneath bare feet in the sunshine, slimy when the water covered it—"Like trailing mermaid's hair," Dolly remarked.

To the children it was their private property, their secret refuge, as was the beach itself below Aunt's house on Pengel Point.

Their mother was dead; their father, the Major, was submerged in his Army career, which was his life, his religion, his total absorption.

Aunt tackled the problem of bringing them up by pretending the submarine did not exist and continuing to live the sort of maidenly, secluded life she had always led.

In trying to adapt themselves to such a life, Tom and Dolly had been thrown inward upon their own resources, storing up within themselves secret, wilful, rebellious feelings. They adopted a general practice of non-communication with the only two grown-ups they knew, and a shell of hatred for the world they did not.

They were by nature fanciful and imaginative, highly strung, with a tendency to deceit and exaggeration, which Aunt called fibbing. And the house and environment did nothing to alter their characters, for it was like a museum, full of old junk, mixed up with pieces of exquisite china and furniture.

The family had lived there for generations and nothing was ever thrown away. In this atmosphere of the decaying past everything had a personality of its own.

When the weather was too bad for them to go out of doors they spent their time in the room which had once been the nursery. It had a deal table and slippery horsehair chairs, covered by a layer of dust. The toy cupboards, their doors hanging from broken hinges, held a wealth of ancient toys from past ancestors, and the lead soldiers and farm animals became characters from the books they had read—*Arabian Nights*, Hans Andersen, *Alice in Wonderland*, and *At the Back of the North Wind*.

But all this was only to pass the time until once more they could get out where the everlasting wind blew on their faces, across the green-clad cliffs, down the rocks, which held the submarine. Here they came alive, king and queen of their own kingdom, rich with endless games from their vivid imaginations.

The favourite was to pretend they were the original crew of the ship, doomed, as they stood in the sun-dappled half-twilight at the base of the rotting ladder, which led up to the conning tower—waiting until the last moment for the running tide, when they would crawl and slither to safety across the rocks of the reef. The sea then soaking them with spray as little tongues of foam crept up the sand creeks, between the black rocks.

The winter storms tore and battered the wreck, gradually tearing pieces of the metal plates away so that each returning spring there was a little less of the rotting hulk left. Its endless fascination lying in the fact that no grown-up ever approached it, did not even know of its existence.

Pengel House stood on a promontory, the beach only accessible by a cliff path. Its nearest neighbour, a mile away, was a building of similar type, which had stood empty for years, until last summer, when it had been bought by the Prison Authority as a home for delinquent boys.

This had brought a spate of letters from Aunt, to Her Majesty the Queen, the Council, and the local Member of Parliament, motivated by her constant fear of prying eyes, intruders and Bolsheviks.

The children ran wild, tanned and weathered like young gypsies, their clothes outmoded, though they were hardly conscious of this, for they never mixed with other children, their education being undertaken by a retired schoolmistress who lived five miles away and came daily by ancient pony and trap.

Miss Bendall had known Aunt since childhood, and although in the latter's opinion, was not quite out of the top drawer, in the absence of any other solution had to be tolerated.

Summer and winter she wore a long tweed skirt and moleskin jacket, her face inches thick in enamel and rouge, for she had been a beauty in her day. She had dyed red hair, surrounding a shining bald spot on the top of her head, which so fascinated Tom that when she bent forward to correct his exercise, he was sorely tempted to challenge Dolly to a game of noughts and crosses on the bare expanse.

The summer holidays were the time they loved best. Long, hot days seemed to stretch endlessly before them, when they swam naked in the bottomless blue of the sea, and lay on the burning sand to dry; until at last, no matter how brightly the sun blazed, they escaped to their secret world within the submarine, with its magic of their own making.

On the lower deck the iron grating, cracked and broken with a jagged hole in the middle, lay scattered with the shale-like plates of the batteries, which had burst from their cases. Here Dolly had once slipped and caught her leg. Tom had had to tug with all his strength to get her free, and all the while the running tide dashed itself on the iron hull.

In a way the sea was their enemy, for it submerged the submarine twice daily, and when the water reached the third rung of the metal ladder, they were forced to clamber up into the sunshine. Reluctantly they would return to the housebound world, where Aunt ignored them, and their father, home on one of his rare visits, would shout at them to "Keep your head up, shoulders back. Stand like men, dammit, not languid lilies!"

They found the boy on a still August day when it seemed as though the sun were motionless, hung like a brass tray in the sky.

After breakfast they had swum and sunbathed, beyond the reef, in the low tide, and then, half tipsy with sun, they climbed the rusty ladder, to creep thankfully into the cool twilit world of the submarine. Dolly had gone first. She gave a little shriek when she saw the pale face, like an open flower, motionless in the depths beneath her. Tom peered over the edge.

"Must be a fish," he said.

Dolly, arrested in her descent, shook her head.

"It's a person, probably a ghost of one of the drowned sailors," she said hopefully.

Warily they climbed down until they stood side by side on the iron grating.

Then they saw it was a boy, not much older than themselves. He lay, half twisted, one leg caught in the jagged edge of iron, his face ghastly in the gloom, his eyes closed. He was breathing in curious little jerks.

"We must wake him up," Dolly said firmly, "get him out of here."

"But he'll tell," Tom said, "he'll tell Aunt. It'll never be our secret place again."

Dolly took hold of the boy's arms and shook him. Beneath her fingers she could feel the bones through the flesh, like a skeleton with no warmth, no life.

The boy opened his eyes, puzzlement and disbelief in them.

"Where the 'ell am I, and who are you?"

Dolly let go his arm. "You're trespassing, you're in our submarine, it's private property. You must go, you've no business here."

The boy tried to move and let out a groan of pain. "It's me leg, it's broke."

"Broken," Dolly corrected, primly, "and it serves you right, you shouldn't be in other people's property."

"I was only 'iding, just for a little while, till they stopped looking for me, then I was going to 'itch a lift to London."

"How did you get to our beach anyway, and who are you hiding from?" Tom asked sternly.

"I'm from the 'Ome, round the cliff," he jerked his thumb vaguely in the direction of land. "Climbed the wall when the fuzz weren't looking. Came down the path. 'Eard them after me, so I runs across to 'ide. Didn't mean no 'arm. Then I slipped on that bloody weed and caught me leg." He looked down at the twisted limb. "Now I suppose I'll have to give meself up."

Dolly sat on the bottom rung of the ladder, chin in hand, watching him as though he were some curious species of animal.

"You'd better go and tell 'em, they'll have to bring a stretcher or something. Maybe a 'elicopter," he said with sudden animation.

"They wouldn't believe us," Tom said, "they never believe anything we tell them. Aunt and Miss Bendall say our heads are full of fancy. We're awful fibbers. Anyway, we shouldn't be allowed to speak to the people at the Home, they're all Bolsheviks, Aunt said so," he added with finality.

The boy's expression changed. "But you must, I can't get out of here else." There was panic in his voice.

"No," Dolly said with deliberation, "you can't. Everyone'll know about this place then, and it's ours, our secret, private place."

His eyes were round with horror, fear, disbelief, his mouth turned down at the corners as though he were about to cry. "That's murder, bloody murder," he said shrilly.

"No one will know," Tom said with cunning; "I told you, no one will believe us."

As he spoke a finger of water crept under the grating. "Tide's turned. Another hour or two and this place'll be under water, then no one'll know about you."

The boy banged his clenched fists on the grating, his voice rising to a scream, "Get me out, get me out, damn and blast you, bloody murderers . . ."

Tom looked at him coolly, "Head up, shoulders back. Don't be a languid lily," he mimicked his father.

Dolly folded her arms and looked stern, "We've already told you, we can't, not even if we wanted to."

Tears ran from the boy's eyes, making channels in the dirt of his thin cheeks. "Please," he whimpered, "please, I'll give you anything you want, anything." He brightened momentarily. "There's probably a reward for finding me!"

Dolly wavered. She'd never seen anyone cry before. Only babies cried.

"How old are you?" she asked with interest.

"Fourteen," he sniffed, wiping his nose on the sleeve of his torn jersey. "Wot's that got to do with it, any road?"

"You're too big to cry. And anyway we don't need the money. We're very rich."

A wave broke against the side of the hull.

"Oh Gawd, get me out of here!" he screamed.

Dolly looked at his leg doubtfully. She bent down and clasped it above the knee, giving it a little tug. The boy shouted in agony.

"You see?" she said with unremitting reason. "It's quite impossible."

"Then don't stand talking about it, go and fetch someone," he moaned. His head fell forwards on his chest as he swung into unconsciousness once more.

The cool, green water lapped round his feet, gently swishing the shingle backwards and forwards.

It had reached the second rung of the ladder.

"Come on, we'd better go," Tom said.

For a few moments Dolly stood looking down at the boy, she nudged him with her toe, but he didn't move. Then she followed Tom up the ladder, out into the warm sunshine, the heat a tangible thing as it quivered and danced on the metal deck.

They turned and looked down at the boy, still and quiet now, his arms spread out like the stems of a pale water-plant in the twilight.

Tom dropped the iron lid of the conning tower with a clang that echoed round the rocks.

Slowly they clambered back to the beach, pausing now and then, glancing back at the submarine.

They climbed the cliff path and sat on the scorched grass, arms clasped round their knees.

Once Dolly thought she heard a thin, high scream, but it was only a wheeling gull uttering its sharp, nostalgic cry at a buzzard, sliding gently down the blue of the sky above the cliff top.

"Come on," Tom said at last, getting to his feet and holding out his hand. "It must be lunch-time, I'm starving."

They turned for a last look at the submarine.

The spray was breaking over the deck.

Soon it would be high tide.

THE SENSORY DEPRIVATION TANK

Celia Fremlin

WITH AN ATTEMPT at nonchalance, Michael leaned down to peer under the heavy soundproof lid which so soon was going to close above him. It was exactly like looking down into his own coffin, and his immediate impulse was to cancel the whole thing, here and now.

But how could he? How could he, Michael Davis, Professor Chilver's star student, be the one to play chicken? If the rest of the class at the Department of Experimental Psychology—well, most of them, anyway—were willing to volunteer themselves as guinea-pigs for this slightly nerve-racking experiment, then who was he to hold back, to let the side down by refusing to volunteer? What would they all think of him?

And above all, what would Fiona think of him when it came to her ears—as it immediately would—that he had ratted out at the last moment? Where then would be her admiration, her romantic vision of him as a latter-day hero?

"I think it's *terribly* brave of you, sweetie!" she'd said, holding his head lightly between her white hands, compelling him to raise his face towards hers, to look right into her greenish, brilliant eyes. "I think you're wonderful—a sort of knight errant performing deeds of derring-do for his lady! A modern, scientific knight errant, of course!" she'd amended, with that small, lightly mocking laugh of hers; and had pulled his face near, nearer, and kissed him full on the lips as if to seal a bargain. As if she knew that for her he would do anything. *Anything.*

A scientific knight errant. Yes, well, it *was* all in the cause of science, naturally. Or—if one were to be cynical—in the cause of furthering Professor Chilver's already glittering reputation by putting to sensational use his latest and most spectacular research toy, the Sensory Deprivation Tank. Long and hard had he battled with the Grants Committee over its installation, and now here it was, a monstrous new appendage to the hitherto unremarkable Psychological Research Laboratory. Sunk below floor level, its great, double lid propped open on metal supports, it looked from above like a cross between an oubliette and a padded cell. Enclosed on all four sides by double soundproofed walls, the interior seemed to have been hollowed out of solid darkness, and to be waiting, in silent expectancy, for its first victim.

Professor Chilver had, of course, explained to his class just what it was that they would be expected to do, and had likewise explained at length the object of the exercise. The idea, roughly, was to explore the effect on the human psyche of total rest in total isolation. Unbroken peace and quiet, in fact.

How much peace and quiet can the average human being actually endure? Inside the warmed and padded interior of the Sensory Deprivation Tank, cut off from all sound, all light, the answer was to be revealed. Lying there in total silence, total darkness and total comfort, the volunteer would find out just how long it was before he went mad: how long, that is, before he began to hallucinate . . . before visions came to him out of the darkness . . . before voices began to babble sinister nonsense out of the silence . . .

Because that was what happened in the end—this was already known from earlier studies. What Professor Chilver wanted to write his new paper on was the nature of these hallucinations, the speed at which they developed in different types of subject, and the extent to which their content related—if at all—to the personality of the subject. He hoped thus to throw fresh—not to say career-boosting—light on the nature of "Stimulus-Hunger". Was it merely a neurotic need in certain types of personality? Or was it truly the case that the human brain does indeed require constant stimulation as decisively and almost as urgently as it needs oxygen? When denied the constant small stimuli—visual, auditory and tactile—of a normal environment, is it compelled, for its own sanity, to conjure up imaginary stimuli out of nothing? Hallucinations, in fact?

An interesting line of enquiry. No wonder so many of the students had been eager to volunteer, in spite of the obvious hazards.

And of course—Professor Chilver had hastened to assure them of this—of course there would be safety precautions, as there always had to be in experiments that involved human beings. At any time, if a subject felt that the experience was becoming more than he could take, all he had to do was to press the button that lay within easy reach of his right hand, and he would instantly be released by the supervisor who would be in constant attendance up above.

"Naturally, no blame will be incurred by such a subject," the professor informed them. "No judgement will be passed upon him." But even as he gave these assurances, a tiny curl of anticipatory scorn was already on his lips, and his steely blue gaze was already raking the uneasy ranks of his students, as if seeking to identify in advance the cowards, the backsliders and the poltroons who would be pressing that button before their allotted span of hours was completed.

"*Some* subjects," he proclaimed evenly, "have been known to press the button within minutes of the lid closing above them. This is referred to as the Precipitate Panic Syndrome; and while—as I have just explained—no penalties will be incurred by this type of reaction, and no judgement will be passed upon it, nevertheless the waste of time and of expensive resources caused by this behaviour pattern is something of which it is impossible to be wholly unaware."

Did Michael imagine it, or did that blue, assessing gaze rest on him a little longer than on any of the others? And if so, how was he being assessed? As a Precipitate-Panic-button-pusher? Or as God's gift to the project, destined to come out with flying colours, crammed with relevant data, and hyped up on just the right kind of hallucinations to support the professor's thesis?

Or could it be—and here Michael was aware of a quite new and unprecedented stab of fear—could it be that that assessing gaze related not at all to his likely performance as an experimental subject, but to something quite, quite different; to something more personal and more damaging even than cracking up on a research project? *Could* it be—could it *possibly* be—that the professor somehow knew about Fiona? About Fiona and Michael, that is, because of course he knew about Fiona. She was his wife.

For a nineteen-year-old student to fall in love with a faculty wife nearly twice his age—this was no rarity on the campus. Nor was it by any means unknown for the faculty wife in question to respond with such abandon, such total lack of discretion, as to ensure that the whole thing rapidly became a public scandal, to the ruination, sometimes, of more than one promising career. But in the case of Fiona and Michael this was out of the question. Fiona's discretion was absolute, and in the art of deception she was a past master, as is not unusual in beautiful and discontented wives nearing the age of forty. Indeed, her skill and ingenuity when it came to dissimulation were so great as to be almost frightening; frightening, sometimes, even to Michael, and even when—as now—these skills were being deployed entirely to his advantage. No way would she have allowed the faintest whisper of their affair to come to the ears of her husband, nor would she have allowed her own behaviour in the home to give him the smallest inkling of what was going on. Famous psychologist he might be, and at the top of his profession, but when it came to psychological manipulation on a personal level, she could run rings round him, and always had done. Well, if a husband has his head in a Sensory Deprivation Tank, it's maybe not so difficult . . . ?

So, no: the professor *couldn't* know anything. Michael realized that he must be imagining that faint air of hostility—and a moment later confirmation of this came when the professor turned to Michael in an unwontedly benign manner and told him that, as the top student of the class, he was to have the honour of doing the first stint in the Sensory Deprivation Tank.

"Eighteen hours will be your assignment this first time," the professor informed him. "We shall start at four-thirty tomorrow —Friday—afternoon, and we shall finish at ten-thirty on Saturday morning. I intend to monitor you myself, so I shall be in the lab throughout this period, to be at hand in case of—well—emergencies. Or in case—though I hardly anticipate this—you should choose to press the panic-button before your time is up . . ." Again, that curl of the lip, that flash of steely-blue contempt; and the interview was over.

Four-thirty. The worst time, really. It gave you almost a whole day of mounting anxiety; breakfast and lunch both ruined by nerves, and tea a non-starter. As the ordeal drew near, Michael found himself going over, yet again, all he had heard or read about these sensory-deprivation experiments; and the more closely he reviewed the data—as yet unnervingly sparse—the less reassuring it seemed.

Absolute darkness; absolute silence—these are things which few people, normally, have ever experienced. On even the darkest night, in even the most closely curtained room, there is always some streak or blur of lesser darkness. In every silence, if you listen carefully, there is always *some* feather-light stirring of vibration against the ear-drum, from near or far. Zero decibels simply don't happen. Except in the Sensory Deprivation Tank?

The darkness, probably, would be the worst. The awful thing about absolute darkness, so some of the early experimenters had reported, was that it was liable to make you panic lest you had gone blind. How, in this total blackness, could you reassure yourself that you had not? Staring, peering this way and that into the darkness, eyeballs at full stretch, desperate for a sensation— some of the volunteers could stand less than a minute of this terror; they pressed the panic-button almost at once, and were released instantly, thankful, disgraced, humiliated, into the blessed light.

Silly, Michael had thought, listening to this sort of scare story; and had indeed said so. The chances that a normal, healthy young person should, by coincidence, happen to go blind at exactly the time when he happened to be taking part in a sensory-deprivation experiment must be so many millions of billions against that— well, it was preposterous. Less, probably, than the chance that the human race might die out because of every baby chancing to be born the same sex as every other, all over the world, for three generations.

"You wait!" they had told him when he'd expounded this bit of armchair logic for their edification: and wait he had, until four-thirty on this soft, sunlit May afternoon.

This was it. Now. He took what felt like his last look at the summer sky, and climbed down into the shadowed cavern. The lid closed with the soft whoosh of a perfect, soundproof fit; the bright line of daylight switched off as by a vast power-cut, a fuse blown at the heart of the cosmos, and he was alone.

The darkness was complete, the silence total; and at once, just as they'd warned him, he began to wonder if he'd gone blind. Yes, in the teeth of all those millions and billions of chances, those preposterous myriads of boy-babies squirming like caterpillars over the face of the earth—in the teeth of all sense, reason, logic, he, Michael Davis, star student of his year, was already panicking lest he had gone blind!

Dark, dark everywhere; his eyes seemed to reach out like stalks, like antennae, scrabbling the blackness for some left-over crumb of light; but there was none. Blind! He closed his eyes to shut out the worst of the dark, at the same time despising himself for such idiot weakness. I must be mad! he scolded himself.

But of course that was another thing. People *did* go mad in these sensory-deprivation experiments, it was a known thing. You could always press the panic-button of course, but how could he, of all people, chicken out like that? And within minutes of being incarcerated, too?

Of course, if he *really* felt he was going mad—but then, how would he know? If you were mad enough to go mad (he told himself confusedly) then you would be mad enough not to recognize your state as madness. You would suppose that the visions looming at you out of the darkness were really there, coming at you, and you would feel that it was only common sense to try and evade them as best you could, flinging yourself from padded wall to padded wall, beating your head against the padded ceiling as you leaped and dodged and tried to fight them off. While up there, in that other world, where the sun still shone and the birds twittered, Professor Chilver would be secretly monitoring your every movement with some devilish device of his own invention, recording your every scream, capturing for all time your idiot reactions to your idiot visions.

The visions. Yes, in the end (so it was reported) almost everyone had visions; and so perhaps it would be better to face them in their early stages, while one could still recognize their unreality?

Cautiously, he opened his eyes into the awful dark, and instantly shut them again, his heart thudding. Out there, on the other side of his eyelids, lay the blindness, waiting to pounce. He wouldn't open his eyes again, oh no. It was too terrifying. For a time, he lay staring at the insides of his eyelids, no longer patterned with the reddish brownish swirls with which he was familiar, but, for the first time he could ever remember, quite dark. And growing darker—he could swear to it.

The total comfort of this padded floor seemed to make it all worse, somehow—more threatening. The human frame, it seems, is no more adapted to total comfort than it is to total darkness, and his hands reached out, panicky, from wall to padded wall, craving a *thing*. Anything. Something to touch. His relief when his fingers encountered the plastic container provided as a non-sensory (as far as possible) "toilet facility" was out of all proportion. A hard thing at last! Unpadded! Cold to the touch! With a rim, too, a real shape, firm and tactile. He ran his fingers around and around it in near-worship. He clutched it to his breast. In the cavern of the shadow of death, the rim, the sharp plastic rim, did comfort him.

How long had he been here? This, he knew, was part of the experiment—to find out about temporal disorientation and the distortion of the time sense. Some of the earlier subjects, so he had learned, had been convinced that they had been immured for two or three days when in fact only an hour had passed. Others, apparently, could hardly believe that their allotted span—eighteen hours, or twenty-four, or even two or three days—had been completed.

"Goodness, I must have been asleep!" they would say. "It only felt like half an hour!"

Half an hour. That's exactly what it *did* feel like, to Michael, now—but what was it *really*? This not-knowing was strangely scarey, and with every minute—every hour—it could only get worse. In a kind of formless, inexplicable panic, he decided from now on to measure out the time in the only way he could—by his own all-too-noticeable heartbeats. Seventy to the minute, wasn't it in the normal resting state? Call it sixty to the minute, for easy calculation, so that when he got to a thousand he would know that a quarter of an hour, or perhaps a little more, had passed. Four thousand to the hour . . . his allotted span of eighteen hours would be over, then, by the time he reached 70,000.

One . . . two . . . three . . . four . . .

Not to open the eyes. No. Just count.

A hundred and seven . . . a hundred and eight . . .

Record it on your fingers, that's the way. Each time you get to a hundred, another finger . . .

One finger . . . two fingers . . . That's the way. Keep going . . .

Michael woke up with a start, and with a sense of utter dismay. He had been *asleep*! He had *lost count*! He had got to—what was it?—over a thousand anyway. At least half an hour that would be—but *then* what had happened? Had he slept for ten minutes? Or ten hours? Or what? He felt himself utterly disorientated, swinging in some abyss of time, infinite in its unmeasurability.

He must find out the time! He must! He must look at his watch, immediately; and in sheer unreasoning panic, he opened his eyes.

Dark, dark, dark! And what's more, the dark had crept closer, somehow, since he had last looked at it, it was right up against his eyeballs now, with nothing in between.

Dark, dark! The craving for some gleam of light was like an illness, he could almost feel the nerve pathways between brain and retina deteriorating, shrivelling from disuse, atrophying; giving up, the miraculous system of carrying messages to the brain closing down for ever.

Even closing his eyes didn't, this time, allay the sense of being blind, for the blindness was lodged now not in the circumambient darkness, but right there, behind his eyes, which screamed for light with the desperation of a starving creature screaming for food.

If it gets worse, said Michael to himself, trying to steady the rocking surge of his dissolving sanity by a clear and deliberate decision; if it gets worse, I shall press the button, and to hell with everybody. In fact, I shall press it *now* . . .

But he did not press it. He dared not. For a thought had come into his mind more terrible than anything yet.

Suppose I press the panic-button and there is no response! Suppose he has just gone off and left me! Just simply gone, fed up with it all! The lab empty . . . locked up for the weekend . . . and me left here, forgotten . . . !

For a moment, so vivid as to be almost a hallucination, he saw the professor's face looming up out of the darkness behind his eyelids—absorbed, intent as always, with the lips pressed close in the familiar thin line of concentration on some recalcitrant but all-absorbing problem. The blue eyes glittered with quiet purpose, as they so often did.

But *what* purpose? Michael felt the sweat break out all over his body. He *knows*! suddenly flashed through his mind. He knows! He is going to leave me here *on purpose*, and never let me out! He is going to ignore the button when I press it, he will let it buzz again and again, scarcely looking up from his work. And when the allotted eighteen hours is over, he is going to pack up his papers in his briefcase, fetch his hat and raincoat from the peg, and lock up the lab for the weekend. He is going to go away and let me die, slowly, in the darkness and the silence, and with the encroaching madness moving in on me. Because he knows. He *knows*; and this is his revenge. He knows, too, that by Monday, when they all come back to the lab, I shall be dead. The air will never last that long . . .

This was madness. This was the onset of paranoia, it must be! And what was this dim and yet insistent thudding noise impinging itself on the silence . . . the place was supposed to be soundproofed, for God's sake! What the hell was it, this thump . . . thump . . . thump? Was it his own heart, beating once more that old tattoo of terror? No, it was his own fists, actually, beating, beating at the padded walls . . .

I'm cracking up, he informed himself, almost coolly, and with a sort of scientific detachment. These are the well-known early symptoms. The next one to be expected will be . . . but before the thought was completed, the next symptom was upon him. The professor's face, mocking, rollicking in the darkness like a mad football, ricocheting from wall to wall, and all around the voices were beginning:

"Out! Out! Out!" they all shrieked, from every direction, and the darkness rocked with the noise, and the voice they all shrieked in was Michael's voice, and while the voices shrieked his hands, too, were busy. All on their own, without consulting him at all, they were slithering this way and that across the padded wall, trying which of them would first reach the panic-button.

It was the right hand that managed to fumble its way there first, and, before Michael could prevent it, it had pounced. It pressed the button; and Michael, like some helpless junior officer, stood alongside, waiting for the world to come to an end.

"Disappointing, Michael!" Professor Chilver pronounced. "Really, most disappointing. Only three and a quarter hours! And I've always thought of you as one of my best students. *Most* disappointing. This is not a criticism, of course, or any kind of judgement. I am a scientist, not a judge. When I say it is disappointing, this is a simple statement of fact . . ."

It was still daylight when Michael finally staggered, humiliated, browbeaten, and still in a state of shock, out of the lab. Like an automaton he moved through the golden summer evening, alive with the bedtime twitterings of birds, to face the worst ordeal of all.

"You mean—you mean you didn't do *anything*!" hissed Fiona, torn between fury and the need, even now, to keep her voice down. "You mean you just pressed the button before time . . . and climbed out as if nothing had happened? You little rat! You cowardly little no-good! So *that's* the end of all our plans!"

It was, too. For ever. Incredulously, now, Michael looked back over the plan—Fiona's plan—as it was supposed to have worked out. At the end of his eighteen hours, when the lid was opened, Michael was to have failed to emerge. He was to have lain there, as if unconscious, until the professor, worried, climbed down to see what was wrong. It would then have been the work of a moment for Michael, by far the younger and more agile of the two, to have sprung to his feet, scrambled out of the contraption, and to have slammed the lid down on the older, much slower man. He, Michael, would then have been the one to ignore the buzzer; to collect his coat from its peg, and to go away, locking up the lab for the weekend. Exactly as in his fantasy, only with the roles reversed . . .

"I couldn't do it!" he mumbled now, not daring to look up. "Of course I hate him—honestly I do, I always have! But I couldn't do it—not to anyone! I just couldn't! Not now that I know what it's like!"

He looked up now, and met the cruel, green, fascinating eyes; and he knew, in that moment, that there was yet another prison, even darker and more terrible than the Sensory Deprivation Tank, from which he must now find a way to extricate himself.

DEATH AT THE BARBECUE

Herbert Harris

THE INVITATION FROM Lady Normanley to an evening garden party was addressed to Anthony Goodman. It was opened, however, by the latter's younger brother Vincent, and Anthony Goodman never had the chance to see it.

Lady Normanley was holding yet another social function of the type to which she had become addicted, a "barbecue party", in the grounds of her large house not far from Dunstable.

The flap of the envelope inscribed "Normanley Hall" was insecurely fastened, and Vincent Goodman, always curious about the activities of his brother, opened it to discover the invitation addressed to Anthony.

Once again he experienced the bitter feeling of hatred born of jealousy and a sense of injustice. Why did it always have to be Anthony who was invited to this kind of social affair? he asked himself. As head of the family publishing business, Anthony, it seemed to him, would go on forever plucking all the plums from life and tossing his younger brother the stones.

He stood for some minutes staring at the invitation, the hate becoming fiercer inside him. His inclination at first was to destroy the invitation and so deny his older brother the opportunity to hobnob yet again with the "right people". But as loathing gave way to cunning, he put the invitation in his pocket, sensing already that he might well turn it to his own advantage.

His brooding presently carried his mind along a train of thought which was both frightening and exciting. It culminated in what he felt quite certain was the really perfect murder plan . . . a plan, he told himself, that was so masterly he just couldn't see how it could fail!

Sitting in his own tiny office in the family business, a room only half as large and half as sumptuous as his brother's, Vincent turned the plan over in his mind. His brain was now racing like a high-powered engine, all the details of the plot falling neatly into place.

He must be careful to be specially nice to Anthony when the latter arrived at his office. Even if Anthony started throwing his weight about, humiliating him, as he often did, he must still not lose his temper or show any signs of animosity. Better to make his last moments happy, anyway; the poor bastard had not much longer to live. He allowed himself a small ironic smile.

On the morning of the day that Lady Normanley's barbecue party was due to take place, Vincent picked up the telephone before his brother arrived at the office and dialled the home of the Normanleys.

When, after a brief delay, a maid brought Lady Normanley to the telephone, he said, "Oh, good morning, Lady Normanley. This is Vincent Goodman speaking, Anthony Goodman's brother. I'm just ringing to say that my brother is very grateful for your kind invitation to the barbecue party this evening, but I'm sorry to say that he won't be able to attend. No . . . you see, he is expecting a very important visitor to his flat in Knightsbridge . . ."

He heard Lady Normanley making politely regretful sounds. Then she said, "Oh, well, it can't be helped, I suppose. Tell your brother I quite understand."

Vincent paused, then went on to say what he had already planned to say: "I do hope you won't think me terribly presumptuous, Lady Normanley, but I've heard so much about your delightful garden parties, and the weather being so warm . . . well, I've been wondering if you would allow me to attend in my brother's place?"

The cultured voice of Lady Normanley rose a key higher. "Why, yes, of course! Do please come along! And please forgive me for not thinking of asking you!"

"Thank you so much," Vincent said warmly. "I shall be looking forward to it tremendously."

Smiling, he replaced the receiver. So far, so good.

A party provided such a wonderful alibi. A dozen or maybe twenty or more highly respected persons would be ready to swear that you were there the whole time, that you were never absent for longer than a few minutes . . .

Yes . . . these impeccable witnesses would confirm that you couldn't possibly have travelled from Dunstable in Bedfordshire to Knightsbridge in London, some thirty-odd miles, murdered somebody, and then returned to the barbecue party at Dunstable, without being absent for a noticeably long time. Whereas his period of absence would amount to hardly any time at all . . .

The scheme was so diabolically clever that the more he thought about it, the better it seemed. It gave him, for the first time, a comfortably warm feeling of superiority over Anthony, who had always considered himself so damned smart.

It surprised him that he felt so little compunction about putting his brother out of the way. But why should he feel sorry? His brother had asked for it, bossing him around for years.

Anthony had deliberately sucked up to Uncle Bernard all along the line. So, of course, when Uncle Bernard died, he had left Anthony complete control of the family publishing company. And how had the precious Anthony reacted to that?

Vincent could remember only too well that degrading interview with his brother, when Anthony had said in his patronizing, sanctimonious manner, "Of course, Vincent, you know that Uncle Bernard never liked you. And then again . . . your getting into trouble at the university and being sent down . . . well, that only made matters worse for you . . .

"However, I suppose I shall have to find something for you to do in the business, though God knows what job you can be trusted with . . ."

Anthony had revelled in his position of power and influence, while he—Vincent—was no more than a glorified office-boy, and could never be anything else until such time as he could step into his older brother's shoes.

That could only happen if Anthony died—or was killed.

Some time after speaking to Lady Normanley, Vincent left his office, walked up the street, and telephoned his brother from a public call-box. Now he had to disguise his voice, a talent he had perfected in college amateur dramatics. He knew he was quite good at it.

"Mr Anthony Goodman? Oh, my name is Cavendish." The voice was cultured, smoothly suave, plummy. "I am Lord Normanley's private secretary . . ."

Anthony's tone of voice changed immediately, becoming sycophantic, toadying. Oh, God, how this miserable swine of a brother loved titles! How he loved to be thought one of the Upper Crust, how anxious he had been always to keep the firm's best clients to himself, excluding everyone else.

"His Lordship would like to see you, sir," Vincent went on in his role of Cavendish. "I think he wishes to talk over a publishing project. He has asked me to ring you and say that he would be delighted if you would call at his house for a drink this evening. You can? Oh, good. You know where we are?"

"Yes, I've met her Ladyship." Anthony was almost drooling.

"His Lordship will be rather late home," Vincent continued in his urbane voice, "so could you possibly make it about nine o'clock?"

"Nine? Yes, of course. I look forward to it very much."

"Excellent. Goodbye, sir."

Vincent was smiling again as he replaced the receiver. Everything seemed to be going to plan.

Later that afternoon, Vincent left his office and returned to his own small and rather insignificant flat at Notting Hill to get dressed for the barbecue party at Normanley Hall.

At around six o'clock he travelled into Bedfordshire by train, finishing the last leg of the journey to Normanley Hall by taxi.

He arrived at Lady Normanley's barbecue party at approximately seven-thirty, the time she had specified on the invitation card. He was immediately taken under the hostess's wing and felt a sense of importance which his brother had never permitted him to feel.

He was soon introduced to the other guests, wandering with groups of them in the garden and around the preparations for the barbecue. He went out of his way to establish his identity and his presence, keeping conspicuously in view of the other guests at all times.

But a few minutes before nine o'clock he slipped away from the rest of the company on the lawn, and concealed himself behind a row of shrubs flanking the gravel drive that led up to the house. He knew that Anthony was a stickler for punctuality, which was, in fact, one of his maddeningly efficient traits.

Making an approximate estimate as to where his brother would pull up, behind some other cars parked there, Vincent waited with a mounting excitement. It was now dark. Lights had appeared on the distant lawn, and there were strains of music floating on the night air.

He realized once again how well his plan was working out when, at almost precisely nine o'clock, Anthony's large and impressive "executive car" came purring up the drive. Vincent tensed himself for action. There was no turning back now.

Anthony's car halted just where his brother had calculated he would stop. Vincent, with silent panther-like movements, padded along behind the screen of shrubs until he drew level with the car.

This was the moment . . . the moment when he was thankful for his superior stature and physique, his earlier preference for sport rather than study . . .

Anthony was seized, swiftly and powerfully, as he stepped from the car. He uttered a brief cry, but that would have been drowned by the music, and the drive was deserted. The arm, wound about his neck from behind, gripped mercilessly, choking the life from him in less than a minute.

Working calmly but quickly, Vincent took the ignition key of the car and pocketed it. He then took from Anthony's jacket the key to the Knightsbridge flat and pocketed that too.

Making sure that his brother was quite dead, he opened the boot of the car, tumbled Anthony's body into it, covered it with a car rug which was conveniently handy, and closed and locked the boot lid quietly.

He then locked the doors of the car, switched off the lights, wiped the sweat from his face, for it was a warm night, and stood for a moment thinking fast, carefully checking over the points of the plan.

Strangulation had been a wise choice. No mess left behind, no telltale traces of blood. The luminous dial of his wrist-watch told him that he had been absent from the party for no more than ten minutes, only the time one would take to visit the cloakroom.

Just as unnoticeably as he had left, he now made his way back to Lady Normanley's spacious lawn, and once again mingled with the guests.

The party showed signs of breaking up at about eleven-thirty, and Vincent Goodman, who had not once left the party except for those dramatic few minutes after nine o'clock, bade his host and hostess good-night.

Presently, attracting not the least attention, he drove away from Normanley Hall in Anthony's car, with his dead brother still under the car rug in the boot.

Now for the final stage of the plan . . .

Drive to Knightsbridge. Park the car in the lock-up garage in the block where Anthony had his flat. Make quite sure nobody was about. After all, it would be the small hours. Carry his brother's body to the ground-floor flat—no problem. Open the flat with Anthony's key. Leave Anthony's body lying on the floor of the flat's bedroom. Perfect.

Just to complete the picture that Anthony had spent the evening in his flat, and had entertained a visitor, he would place some bottles and a couple of glasses (wearing gloves to avoid leaving prints) on a trolley in the lounge.

And, of course, there would be the testimony of Lady Normanley: "Vincent Goodman told me his brother was expecting a visitor, which was why he came in Anthony's place . . ."

Vincent knew they would question him as to who the visitor might have been. But he could answer, "I'm afraid I haven't the faintest idea, as my brother never told me anything about his private life." Which would be quite true.

The forensic experts would say he had been killed by strangulation at approximately nine o'clock. The motive? Did he have homosexual friends? Vincent smiled at the thought. Of course, he himself was a suspect, but completely ruled out . . .

Between seven-thirty and eleven-thirty Vincent Goodman was a guest at a barbecue party at Lady Normanley's residence near Dunstable in Bedfordshire. And on no occasion had he been absent long enough for him to travel to Knightsbridge, kill his brother and return to the party. Yes, a clean sheet! God, it had been a masterly idea! What could possibly go wrong?

*

The newspapers, knowing nothing yet about the Perfect Plan, merely reported initially:

"At St. Mary's Hospital, St. Albans, detectives wait to take a statement at the bedside of publishing executive Vincent Goodman, driver of a car which late last night collided with a truck that crossed the central reservation of the M1 motorway.

"A passenger, Anthony Goodman, the driver's brother, was dead when taken from the car, but doctors at the hospital were said to be uncertain as to the cause of the man's death and police were called in early this morning."

MURDER À LA MODE

Richard Grayson

"AS YOU CAN see, Monsieur, the lady's neck is broken. She was also beaten with considerable force."

The doctor pulled the sheet back up to cover the dead woman's face. Inspector Gautier had seen the face many times before, but at a distance. Odette de Fresneau was one of the leading cocottes in Paris, the great "horizontales" as they were often called. Together with Liane de Pougy and Caroline Otero, she was one of a triumvirate of beautiful ladies who had ruled the demi-monde since the turn of the century. Men squandered fortunes over them, fought duels for them, and one at least had blown his brains out when his attempts to buy their favours had been rejected.

Before leaving the bedroom with the doctor, Gautier looked around him. Apart from the bed, which was crumpled and in places stained with blood, there were no signs of a struggle. A man's tail-coat, starched collar and white bow tie were draped over a chair, while the long green gown that Odette must have been wearing lay, together with her underclothes, on the floor beside the bed. A magnificent emerald and diamond necklace lay tossed carelessly on the bedside table.

Outside in the drawing room three people were waiting; a heavy, middle-aged man who sat slumped in a chair, a dark-skinned girl in a dressing gown, and Surat, the inspector's assistant. The girl was Odette's maid, an Arabian named Yasmin, and it was she who had called the doctor and the police when she found her mistress dead. She had a very pretty face and had heightened the colour of her cheeks with rouge, as well as using kohl to darken her eyelids and emphasize the almost startling brilliance of her eyes. At a time when the use of cosmetics was barely accepted, and then only by

ladies of fashion who felt that their complexions could not stand
up to the merciless exposure of the new electric lighting, it was
unusual to find a maid using colour on her face. But then it was the
Arabians, Gautier remembered reading, who were supposed to
have introduced these colouring artifices into Europe.

The middle-aged man's face was also known to the inspector.
He was a prince of a neighbouring country who visited Paris
regularly, never attempting to conceal that what he enjoyed most in
the pleasure capital of the world was not the food nor the wine nor
the gaiety, but the women. His name had been linked not only with
the great courtesans but with actresses, circus riders and even the
dancers of the Moulin Rouge. In spite of these amorous escapades,
or perhaps because of them, the prince had become immensely
popular in France, and many Frenchmen even tried to imitate his
style of dress and beard and walk. Over the past year or two this
popularity had done much to improve relations between his
country and France, which for many generations had been soured
by hostility and suspicion. Now Gautier saw the prince, dressed
only in his evening shirt and trousers, apparently stupefied by
drink.

He had heard the maid's story at second hand from a policeman
stationed at the nearby commissariat of the ninth arrondissement,
who had been called to Odette's apartment, and who in turn had
sent a message to Sûreté headquarters, where Gautier had been
on night duty. Her mistress, she had said, had returned from
dining at Maxim's with the prince and two other gentlemen, the
Comte de Trèves and Monsieur Boris Gratz, both of them old
friends of Odette's. Yasmin had served them champagne and had
then been told that she could go to bed. Shortly after three a.m. she
had gone into Odette's bedroom and found her mistress dead and
the prince lying in a drunken stupor beside her.

"Where is your bedroom?" Gautier asked the girl.

"Two storeys up on the top floor of the building, Monsieur. The
servants of all the families with apartments here have rooms on
that floor."

"And why exactly did you come down to Madame's apartment
at that hour?"

Yasmin told him she had been woken from sleep by a

frightening dream in which she had seen her mistress crying for help as she was being attacked by a man. The dream had made such an impression on her that she had got out of bed and come downstairs to peep into Odette's bedroom, just to reassure herself that her mistress was all right. Gautier made no comment. Magic, the occult and telepathy were all the rage in France then, and he had heard of similar instances when people had been warned of danger in dreams. After making the girl tell him where her bedroom was situated, he told her to return to bed.

When he and Surat had arrived from the Sûreté a few minutes previously, they had been admitted to the building by a policeman who had been posted outside by the local commissariat, but he had noticed the concierge, an elderly woman, sitting in the room which she occupied just inside the entrance. The room was directly opposite the staircase that led to the upper floors of the building, and it was the concierge's responsibility to open the main door to any residents or visitors who might arrive after it had been locked for the night. Gautier told Surat to accompany the doctor downstairs on his way out of the building, and then to question the concierge and find out whether she could confirm Yasmin's story.

The prince, who had fallen asleep in his chair, was snoring with a hissing noise that resembled an escape of gas, and bubbles of saliva had formed on his lips. Gautier had already decided not to ask him any questions until his secretary arrived. The secretary, himself of noble blood and a colonel in the army, was staying with the prince in an expensive but discreet hotel in the Rue de Rivoli, which they always occupied on private visits to Paris, and a messenger had been sent from the Sûreté to tell him what had happened.

While he was waiting for Surat to return he noticed, standing on a table beyond the prince's chair, four champagne glasses and an empty bottle that had once held Mumm champagne. Two bottles of the same marque, also empty, had been placed upturned in a champagne bucket that was half full of melted ice. More through curiosity than for any definable purpose, he picked up one of the glasses and sniffed at it. In search of exotic sensations, some decadent members of Paris society, he knew, would sometimes add a few drops of ether to their drinks, but he could smell nothing but champagne. Three of the four glasses held the dregs of what had been drunk from them, but the fourth was empty. Turning it upside-down he saw that it was completely dry.

Presently Surat returned from speaking to the concierge. He told Gautier that the woman could be of little help to them. She could recall a gentleman calling in a carriage to take Madame de Fresneau to dinner and had a hazy recollection of admitting them to the building later at night with other guests, but she could not say how many guests there had been nor who they were. She could not remember anyone at all leaving the building afterwards.

"Has the woman been bribed to hold her tongue?" Gautier asked.

"I don't think so, patron. It's simply that she's very, very drunk."

"A drunken concierge? That doesn't sound very satisfactory."

"There was a bottle of fine old cognac in her place, almost empty. If you ask me she has drunk the lot tonight. I was going to take it away from her but she began shouting abuse at me; said it was her present, a little present from a friend."

"We can question her again when she's sober. In the meantime I want you to go and fetch the Comte de Trèves and Monsieur Boris Gratz. Neither lives far away; the comte in Rue de Monceau and Gratz in Avenue des Champs Elysées. Tell them I wish to question them and ask them to accompany you here."

"At this hour? They may not be willing to come."

"Tell them I insist. If they refuse, they will be taken before a juge d'instruction tomorrow morning."

Surat left, wondering, no doubt, why his superior could not wait until the morning to question the drinking partners of the prince and Odette. He was an excellent policeman, loyal and efficient, but he had not realized, as Gautier had, that if the prince had murdered one of Paris's best-known cocottes it would create a scandal of enormous proportions with diplomatic repercussions. If, on the other hand (however unlikely it might seem), the prince was innocent, then it was important that the murderer should be identified and apprehended before the story became public and the newspapers of the world began publishing their speculations and scurrilous innuendoes.

Shortly after Surat had departed, the prince's private secretary arrived. The colonel had dressed quickly after he had been roused from his bed, putting on the first clothes that came to hand, and he was wearing a belted travelling jacket with the trousers of his evening suit. He had been told by the messenger from the Sûreté only that the prince had been found in a dangerously compromising situation, and when he came into the room Gautier quickly filled him in with the facts.

"Monsieur l'Inspecteur, it is inconceivable that His Highness should have killed this woman," the colonel exclaimed when Gautier had finished speaking. "He is the most courteous and gentle man I know. The prince would never strike a woman, nor use any form of violence, if it comes to that."

"Not even when he has drunk too much?"

"Never!"

Gautier knew that what the colonel was saying was not wholly true. Although the prince paid extravagant compliments to women, lavished gifts on them, and had the reputation of being a gallant, considerate lover, there had been from time to time in his life incidents, only partially hushed up, which suggested that his temper was not always under control. Once in Paris a dancer from the Elysée Montmartre had tried to sue him for assault, complaining that he had broken her nose and knocked out two of her teeth. But there was nothing to be gained from arguing with the colonel, who was as loyal to the prince as he was devoted, so he asked another question.

"Had His Highness known Madame de Fresneau for long?"

"No. He saw her for the first time a few days ago when he was riding in the Bois de Boulogne."

"But this was their first rendezvous?"

"No; he arranged a meeting with her through an intermediary two nights ago."

"Then we may assume that she pleased him, as he met her again so soon."

"I presume so."

"Well, perhaps we had better wake him and see what he has to say."

Together and with some difficulty they roused the prince. Even when his eyes were finally open they had a dull, uncomprehending look, and he made no reply to Gautier's first question, but stared at them stupidly.

"Your Highness, I implore you, answer us," the colonel pleaded. "How was the woman killed?"

"Killed? Who has been killed?" The prince's heavily accented French was slurred.

"Madame de Fresneau. You dined with her earlier this evening, sir. Remember?"

The prince shook his head and said, "What are we doing here?"

Gautier made a sudden decision. "We'll learn nothing from His Highness tonight," he told the colonel. "Take him back to your hotel and I'll come round to see you tomorrow morning."

"Will the public hear of this? The newspapers?"

"Inevitably. An affair like this cannot be kept secret."

"You know that the prince is in Paris incognito?"

"Yes, but his name cannot be concealed for long. He is too well known in France. And of course if he did kill the woman—" Gautier left the sentence unfinished.

They looked at the prince and saw that he was not even listening to what was being said. His eyes were closing again, his head swaying. The colonel said, "In that case the scandal would destroy him. It could even be the end of monarchy in my country."

"Aren't you exaggerating, Colonel?"

"Not at all. The admiration which you French have for him would turn to odium and your government would almost certainly reject the proposed alliance, an alliance which our country badly needs. Don't forget we have a radical government which is already ill-disposed towards royalty."

"We will know the truth soon enough," Gautier said. "In the meantime, Colonel, take the prince to your hotel. I will have two men posted outside the entrance to protect you from reporters and other busybodies."

"You have been most considerate, Monsieur." The colonel nodded his head politely, although he knew that the two policemen outside their hotel would also be on duty to make sure that he and the prince did not leave the country hastily.

Boris Gratz had dressed more carefully than the colonel and his tail-coat and white evening shirt were as neat and fresh as though he had just put them on to go out for the evening. Gautier had never met the man before, but had seen his name often enough in the society columns of *Figaro*. A Mid-European by birth, Gratz was one of the new cosmopolitan set that had been drawn to Paris as the most civilized and sophisticated capital in Europe and had made their home there. He was a bachelor in his late forties and had a magnificent house, two fine carriages, and a stable of Arab horses, on one of which he could often be seen riding in the Bois. Handsome, witty, and a patron of the arts, he was in great demand by the hostesses of the "gratin" or upper crust. He was also an able businessman who represented an American firm of armament manufacturers and had just sold a revolutionary new rifle to the French Ministry of War.

"When your man told me Madame de Fresneau had been murdered, I could not believe it," he told Gautier. "She and the prince were so happy in each other's company. They were entranced with each other. It was love at first sight, a real *coup de foudre*."

"Your disbelief suggests that you think he must have killed her."

Gratz shrugged his shoulders. "Your assistant tells me they were found together in her bed, Odette dead and the prince covered in blood."

"The facts indicate that he may well have killed her, but we must examine all possibilities."

"Of course. I can see that."

"Tell me, Monsieur, how did it happen that the four of you were together this evening? Did you and the Comte de Trèves meet the others by arrangement?"

"No, it was sheer chance. I had persuaded the comte to visit the Cirque d'Été with me. I thought the beautiful lady riders there might distract him; take his mind off his disappointment."

"What disappointment?"

"As you may have heard, Odette and he were the closest of friends for a year or more; then recently they agreed to end their liaison."

What Gratz did not say, but thousands of newspaper readers

knew, was that the Comte de Trèves's affair with the cocotte had ended when his father, the Duc de Linteuil, had threatened to disinherit his son if he did not give up Odette. The reason for the duc's ultimatum was that the comte had in a rash moment given Odette an emerald and diamond necklace which had been owned by the family, handed down to each succeeding eldest son and intended for his wife. The comte had no right to give the family heirloom away and at his father's insistence had tried to persuade Odette to return it, but she had refused. There was talk of legal action but the comte's family were reluctant to face the scandal that would follow.

Gratz told Gautier that he and the comte had left the circus before the performance was over and gone to Maxim's, where they had found the prince dining with Odette and another couple. The prince, who had often met Gratz sailing and at the races, had invited the two of them to join his party and later the four of them had returned to Odette's apartment for a final glass of champagne to end the evening.

"One would think it could hardly console the comte to spend an evening with his former mistress and her new lover," Gautier observed.

"Oh, he's no longer lovesick." Gratz smiled. "One has to accept reality in these matters."

As they were speaking they heard the front door of the apartment open and Surat came in accompanied by the Comte de Trèves himself. In appearance the comte and Gratz had much in common. They were both tall, slim and fair, with moustaches that had been carefully trimmed and waxed, but one could detect in the comte's physique, in the bone structure of his face, and in his bearing a hint of effeminacy, the legacy perhaps of generations of close breeding.

"It was good of you to come so promptly, Monsieur le Comte," Gautier greeted him.

"I cannot believe that Madame de Fresneau has been murdered," the comte replied, shaking his head.

His words were so similar to those Gratz had used when he had arrived a few minutes earlier, that Gautier wondered for a moment whether they were speaking to an agreed and rehearsed script. He put the idea from his mind, reminding himself that one should never grasp at premature suspicions until the facts had all been assembled.

"Monsieur Gratz has kindly explained how you and he came to meet up with the prince and Madame de Fresneau. What I would like to know is at what time you both left this apartment."

"We didn't leave together," the comte replied. "I stayed on after he left for a short time."

"I see. And do you know at what time you did finally leave?"

"I arrived home shortly after two o'clock," Gratz said helpfully.

"Did you have a carriage waiting here?"

"No. We let my coachman go at Maxim's. When I left here I found a *fiacre* at the corner."

Gautier turned to the comte. "Were the prince and Madame de Fresneau sober when you left?" His question clearly embarrassed the comte, so he added, "You may as well be frank, Monsieur. When I arrived the prince appeared to be very, very drunk."

"They had both been drinking. We all had."

"Did you quarrel with Madame de Fresneau?" Gautier asked bluntly. "Or with the prince?"

The comte flushed. His expression was not one of resentment at being asked the question, but of brooding ill-will, as though it had aroused a memory which he had wished to put behind him. "Certainly not!"

"Then let me put you another question. Why did you stay on here after your friend left?"

"There was a matter which I wished to discuss with Madame de Fresneau."

"Would that have been the return of your family's necklace?"

"Really, Inspector!" Gratz protested. "That's a private matter!"

"It's all right, Boris," the comte said wearily. "All Paris knows about the necklace, so why shouldn't the Sûreté know too. Yes, that's what I wished to discuss, and it seemed an opportune occasion for this reason."

The comte had decided, he told Gautier, to make one last approach to Odette that night to return the necklace, because he believed the prince might take his side in the affair and use his influence to persuade Odette to be more reasonable. A prince would understand about family obligations and how in a reckless moment a man might make an extravagant gesture and give away something that was not his to give. In the event his plan had failed. Odette had continued to be stubborn and the prince had declined to become involved in the argument at all, seeming embarrassed and annoyed that it should have even been mentioned in his presence.

"Was she wearing the necklace?" Gautier asked.

"She would never have been so tactless," Gratz said.

"It would appear that you left the apartment at about two o'clock. Did the concierge let you out of the building?"

"Yes."

"I'm surprised she was able to. She seems very drunk."

"I had to help her open the door," the comte admitted, "she could scarcely put the key in the lock."

"You have been a regular visitor here. In your experience was the concierge often drunk?"

"From time to time, yes. Drunk but not incapable. As you know, Inspector, many concierges drink too much. They have nothing to do through long hours of waiting except to knit or sew and keep sipping wine."

"One last question, Monsieur le Comte. Did you form the impression that His Highness and Madame de Fresneau were still on good terms when you left them?"

"Let me put it this way." The comte's reply was edged with bitterness. "Neither of them tried to stop me leaving. They could hardly wait to get to bed."

Gautier moved towards the door which separated the room in which they were from Odette's bedroom. At the same time he nodded at Surat to indicate that he could accompany him. He told the comte and Gratz, "Gentlemen, I must ask you to excuse me for a few moments. My assistant and I have an investigation to make. If you would be so kind as to wait until we return, then I believe this matter can be resolved."

"What are we looking for, patron?" Surat asked Gautier when they were in the bedroom. "And where shall we start searching?"

"We don't need to search." As he replied Gautier crossed the room to the table by the bed, picked up the emerald and diamond necklace which lay there and handed it to Surat. "I want you to put this in your pocket and keep it there."

Surat did as he was told. He never questioned any of Gautier's instructions, however bizarre they might seem, even by a raised eyebrow. He knew from experience that his superior never gave orders either on a mere whim or simply to demonstrate his authority.

"I came in here partly to marshal my thoughts," Gautier said, "but also to give those two gentlemen time to lose a little of their irritating complacency."

"Does that mean you believe they are implicated in killing this woman?" Surat nodded towards the body beneath the sheet.

"Why not?"

"On the surface it looks as though the prince must have killed her; not intentionally, perhaps, but in a drunken frenzy."

"Then how do you explain that the necklace, which Odette had not been wearing, should be lying on the table by the bed?"

"When they came in here the prince may have been curious to see the necklace over which so much fuss was being made."

"From the way in which Odette's clothes had been just dropped on to the floor, he had only one thing in mind."

Gautier did not add that there were other aspects of the affair which were puzzling him; small questions, none of which would seem significant in itself, but which taken together demanded an answer. He wished to know, for example, why the maid Yasmin had been wearing cosmetics, and why one of the four champagne glasses on the table seemed not to have been used, and why a concierge should be drinking fine old cognac. He did not mention these questions to Surat. Instead he thought out the plan he was going to put into operation.

Finally he said, "It's time we rejoined the comte and Monsieur Gratz. And I want you to go downstairs. The man from the Sûreté who brought the prince's secretary here is waiting by the concierge's lodge. Bring him and the policeman from the local commissariat up here."

The comte and Gratz were still in the drawing room where he had left them. Neither of them appeared resentful or impatient at being kept waiting. Both had lit cigars, and the air in the unventilated room, already stale, was thick and oppressive.

"Were your investigations rewarding, Inspector?" One could detect a hint of irony in Gratz's question.

"Yes. They confirmed what I already suspected, that the prince did not kill Madame de Fresneau."

It was Gratz who reacted more quickly to Gautier's statement. "How can that be? We were told he was found lying by her dead body."

"That is true."

"Are you saying he lay there while someone else brutally attacked and killed her?"

"Yes. You see, I believe the prince was drugged."

"That's absurd. He never took drugs."

"Possibly not, but a strong sleeping draught could easily have been put in his champagne."

Gratz's face hardened, but he kept his feelings under control. "Are you accusing us of drugging the prince as part of a plot to kill Madame de Fresneau?"

"Not you, Monsieur, but the Comte de Trèves."

The comte stared at Gautier. His eyes were frantic, as his mind, like a bird trapped in a drawing room, searched for a way to escape but found none.

"This is just a theory you have invented for political expediency, Inspector," Gratz said, and the first signs of anger appeared in his voice, "to protect the prince. You cannot possibly believe that the comte would kill Odette, callously and in cold blood."

"Why not? It is an explanation that fits the facts. As he has admitted, the comte stayed on here after you left. Perhaps he did ask Madame de Fresneau to return his necklace, but he had come prepared to kill her if she refused." Gautier turned to the comte and asked him, "You knew she kept the necklace here, didn't you?"

"Yes. She would never lodge it with any bank, because she was afraid my family might persuade the bank to return it to them."

"When you saw that the sleeping draught you had put into the prince's champagne was taking effect," Gautier continued, "you pretended to leave. But you waited outside the apartment until the lovers had time to get into bed, then you came back, killed Madame de Fresneau, left her lying there beside the prince and went home. You had already sent the concierge a bottle of cognac, knowing she was a drunkard and that she would be too drunk to see if your clothes were bloodstained when you left the building."

"Are you saying I killed Odette to get the necklace back?" the comte demanded.

"Yes."

"But I haven't got the necklace. It must still be here!"

"We have only your word for that, Monsieur. One thing I do know. It is not anywhere in the bedroom."

"Then someone else must have taken it."

Ignoring the comte's protests, Gautier crossed the room to the door. Outside, in the entrance hall of the apartment, Surat was waiting with the two policemen, and he beckoned them into the room. It was a piece of pure theatre and unlikely to achieve any dramatic effect, but it could do no harm, and privately he rather enjoyed acting.

"Monsieur le Comte," he said with a grave air. "I must ask you to accompany these policemen."

"Where?"

"They will send for a police wagon and in it take you to Sûreté headquarters where you will be detained until the morning when you will be brought before a juge d'instruction."

Faced with the humiliation of arrest and prison, the comte's manner changed dramatically. The whole elaborate structure of his dignity and pride and self-assurance collapsed, and as it did his features too appeared to change. His good looks and youth and vanity decomposed into shame. Without speaking he accompanied the two policemen out of the room, leaving Gratz alone with Gautier and Surat.

"This is monstrous!" Gratz exclaimed, and he was unmistakably angry now. "You have no evidence against the comte to justify arresting him!"

Gautier shrugged his shoulders. "If he did kill Madame de Fresneau, we will have all the evidence we need after he has been before the magistrate. He is not a man who could withstand interrogation."

"If the prince had not been involved, you would never have arrested him." As he was speaking Gratz stood up. "Your conduct in this business cannot be tolerated. I shall go now, even at this hour, to the home of the Minister of Justice and secure his release."

"You must do as you please, Monsieur."

"What do we do now?" Surat asked when he and Gautier were alone. "I suppose we should arrange for the body to be taken to the mortuary."

"The doctor promised to see to that. The mortuary attendants should be here at first light."

"Do you wish me to stay until they arrive?"

"No. Our night's work is not yet done," Gautier replied. "Come with me."

Surat followed him out of the apartment, thinking that they might be going to question the concierge in the hope that she might now be sober. Instead Gautier led him upstairs, continuing up the winding staircase until they reached the top storey of the building, where the rooms of the domestic servants were to be found. They arrived in a narrow corridor, lit only by a single gas jet at each end and seeming even dingier than it was because of the low ceiling.

"Will she still be awake?" Surat asked, assuming that they were going to question the maid, Yasmin.

"I'm sure she will," Gautier replied, and he smiled as he added mockingly, "but let us proceed as quietly as we can just in case."

Yasmin had pasted a rectangular piece of white card on the door of her room, and it bore her name, written in an elaborate, curling script within a carefully drawn border of leaves and flowers in the style of "art nouveau", which was then the rage in Paris. Gautier stopped outside the door for a moment and stood silently with his ear pressed to the panels. Then he threw it open and strode into the room.

The maid was sitting up in bed. The nightdress she was wearing showed off her bare brown shoulders and did nothing to conceal her rounded breasts. Her voice was raised in anger or indignation, but she left whatever she was saying unfinished, choking back the words when Gautier and Surat burst in. Standing over the bed, looking down at her, was Boris Gratz.

"You're wrong, Monsieur," Gautier told Gratz. "It was not she who took the necklace."

"What?" Gratz stared at him.

"Show it to him, Surat."

Taking the necklace from his pocket, Surat held it up. Yasmin looked at it and then said to Gratz, "You see! Now do you believe me?"

"Hold your tongue!" Gratz shouted at her.

"Don't listen to him, Mademoiselle," Gautier said. "By talking you may save yourself, if not from prison, then at least from the guillotine."

The mention of the guillotine had a shattering effect on Yasmin. Her mouth fell open and she began to tremble. He went on, "Of course you cannot deny that you helped him in his plan to kill your mistress, but a jury might believe he used you."

"You're mad!" Gratz had been shaken too but he was recovering his composure. "First you accuse the comte, now me."

Ignoring his interruption, Gautier told the girl, "You can tell us how it happened, how he warned you that he and the comte would be coming back with your mistress and the prince, how he would pretend to leave before the comte and come here to hide in your room; then after the comte had left he would go down and kill your mistress in a way which would incriminate the prince. Tell us what he offered you to be his accomplice. Money? Or did he promise to make you his mistress, to set you up in an apartment of your own, introduce you to the gentlemen of Paris? Perhaps he was your lover already."

"Don't say anything!" Gratz ordered the girl. "Can't you see he's only guessing?"

Yasmin did not seem to hear him. She said quickly, "Yes, that's how it was. He made me all sorts of promises. He made me help him."

Suddenly losing control, Gratz bent down and struck her across the face, then grabbed her throat with his hands. Gautier leapt forward, and he and Surat dragged Gratz away from the bed and after a struggle overpowered him. As he fought he screamed obscenities at them.

"You must accompany us to the Sûreté," Gautier told Yasmin. "Get dressed and come downstairs to the conciergerie."

They took Gratz, still struggling and cursing, downstairs, where they found the Comte de Trèves and the two policemen who were escorting him still in the concierge's lodge, for the police wagon had not yet arrived. Gautier gave instructions for the comte to be released and then apologized to him, explaining what had happened after he had been taken away from Odette's apartment.

"Was the charade you played really necessary?" the comte asked. His only concern was for his wounded pride, and he showed no surprise that his friend Gratz had committed a brutal murder.

"It was the only way I could prove that Gratz had conspired with the girl," Gautier replied. "And it worked far better than I had hoped. I was sure you would not mind my little deception, Monsieur, if it helped us to find out who had killed Madame de Fresneau."

The comte left to find a *fiacre* and presently the horse-drawn police wagon drew up in the street outside the building. The two policemen took Gratz and the maid into the wagon, the doors were locked and the horses ambled away. Justice in France, Gautier reflected, was as leisurely as the horses pulling the wagon, and Gratz would have plenty of time to regret his abortive plan before he was brought to trial in the great Assize Court at the Palais de Justice.

"I shall walk back to headquarters," he told Surat.

"May I come with you, patron?"

"Of course."

They walked through the deserted Place de la Concorde and along the right bank of the Seine, intending to cross to the Ile de la Cité by Pont Neuf. Although it was still night, the sky to the east was a perceptibly paler shade of dark blue, and in not much more than an hour Paris would be stirring. Behind them stood the Eiffel Tower and in front the twin towers of Notre Dame, the one a symbol of the new self-assertive France that had arisen out of the ruins of defeat by Germany, the other a monument to her centuries of civilization.

"Why did Gratz kill the woman?" Surat asked as they walked.

"Who knows? Money, power, politics are all so closely related that one cannot disentangle them. Had the prince been arrested for the murder of Odette, the French government would have been forced by public opinion to withdraw from the proposed alliance with his country. Many other governments in Europe would give much to see that happen. Gratz is a businessman with contacts at the highest level in many countries. Besides, the alliance would stabilize the balance of power in Europe and the danger of war would have receded. War, no doubt, is what Gratz wants most of all. Think of all the guns he could sell!"

"But why did he involve the Comte de Trèves?"

"The comte was central to his plan. It was he who would confirm that Gratz had left the apartment when Odette was still alive. The only danger was that he might himself be suspected of killing Odette to get his necklace back. That was why Gratz found the necklace and left it lying where it would immediately be seen. When I told him it was not in the bedroom, he at once concluded that the maid had been carried away by greed and had taken it. If he had been able to make her admit she had taken it, we would have had to release the comte."

"And arrest the prince? Ingenious!"

"Too clever. The crime of a gifted amateur. One can excuse him for forgetting to pour a little champagne back into the glass from which the prince had drunk after he had cleaned and dried it. One can even understand why he would have sent the concierge a bottle of cognac from his own cellar instead of absinthe, which would have got her drunk even quicker and been more in character. If he had gone out to buy a bottle or sent out for one, it might have been traced to him. But allowing Yasmin to keep paint on her face when she was supposed to be coming down straight from a nightmare to find her mistress dead was unforgivable!"

CAST FOR MURDER

Kenneth Benton

IN FACT, I'M the last person to think of murder as a solution to any problem. My sister Rosie, with that slightly mocking smile which I know so well, says I'm a gentle creature, and so I am, as a rule. But my hatred of Bill Rodgers, Rosie's husband, had been smouldering for some time, because I knew how much she must be suffering. I couldn't allow that to go on.

Rosie and I were orphaned early. She is a good deal younger than I am, and I've always loved and protected her. For me, there's never been any other woman. But when Bill was transferred here as bank manager she fell in love with him overnight—and I use the word deliberately, since they met at a dance and she didn't come creeping in until five in the morning, to find me out of my mind with anxiety and on the line to the police.

I had hated the idea of her marrying anybody, but if she had to, he wasn't a bad choice, I suppose. Bill was a good-looking chap and well liked, and he obviously adored Rosie. But then, so did everybody; that was the trouble. At least he was a fly-fisher, and almost up to my standard which, as you can see from my row of pots, is quite high.

Rosie still came in two days a week to help in the shop—I'm a bookseller—and since she got on well with my sub-manager, a cheerful rugger-player named Gavin, we managed nicely.

All went well with the marriage, even to my jaundiced eye, for nearly two years. But then things began to go wrong. I'd called on Bill one Sunday morning, to go fishing. Even before the door was opened I could hear them quarrelling. Rosie's face was flushed.

"Are you all right?" I asked anxiously.

"Of course," she snapped. "We were only having an argument."

Bill said nothing. On our way to the lake I ventured, "I don't like to see you and Rosie scrapping, Bill. Is there anything I can do?"

"No, Ray, there isn't," he said rather brusquely. "Your sister's got to learn a lot about marriage."

"Perhaps you have, too," I retorted.

"Perhaps." He relapsed into silence.

Next morning she was working in the shop and I called her into my office to have coffee. She seemed anxious not to talk about Bill, but I insisted. "Do you often have these tiffs?"

She smiled ruefully. "It was a bit more than a tiff, Ray." She was pouring my coffee as she spoke, and I saw a mark half hidden by the short sleeve of her blouse. She caught my eye and hurriedly pulled down the sleeve. "What's that bruise on your arm?" I demanded.

"It's nothing, Ray."

"Let me see." I seized her hand and pushed back the sleeve. There were the clear blue marks of fingers on her arm. She struggled, but I held her firmly and discovered similar marks on the other arm. I felt sick, and could hardly speak. The thought of another man touching her had been bad enough; that anyone should deliberately hurt her was unbearable. "Did Bill do this?" I asked harshly.

She stared at me, hesitating, her eyes wide. "Yes," she whispered.

"Has he done this before?"

Another pause, then, "Yes, Ray. But it doesn't matter. This is nothing."

"*Nothing*? What else has he done to you, for God's sake?"

"He's—he's a bit rough with me sometimes, Ray," she muttered. Then she added quickly, fixing me with wide, candid eyes. "I still love him, though."

I rose. "I'm going to have a talk with your precious husband."

"No," she said quickly. "No, Ray darling, you mustn't do that. Promise me you won't. He'd be—I'd be scared."

By this time I was beside myself with rage. "You can come and live with me again," I said, to comfort her. "I'm going to have it out with him now."

She was in front of me before I could reach the door. "You mustn't, Ray. Give me time. I'll make him see I'm trying to be a good wife to him. Swear you won't say anything to him now. *Swear it!*"

I've always done what Rosie wants. I promised, and she threw her poor bruised arms around my neck and kissed me.

A week later Gavin told me casually, "Rosie's got a black eye, poor girl. I saw her coming out of Boots."

I felt my heart pounding. "*A black eye?*"

"Yes. She said she'd banged into the bathroom door. It seems a funny thing to do."

It wasn't funny to me. It was Bill's doing, and I saw red. It was my own sister he was hitting. What right had he got to touch her? I rang Rosie and begged her to leave him and live with me again. She refused, laughing, and insisting that the black eye was due to the door. I didn't believe her.

That night I couldn't sleep. Ugly thoughts kept churning through my head. I couldn't bear the thought that this brute would go on ill-treating her unless I stopped him. As the hours wore on I formed a plan. I *could* stop him, and for good.

I had a rusty old anchor in my garage weighing about twenty pounds, which I thought would be just right. I changed the line on my salmon rod for one with a high breaking strain and tied to the trace a tiny grapnel I'd made up by lashing three trout flies together. Then I rang Bill and made a date to go fishing.

When we met I had the anchor wrapped up in the stiff oilskins I wear in bad weather. Bill laughed at me for being a pessimist.

We rowed our boats to the middle of the lake, where the bottom is very deep and where Bill fancies the fish are less sophisticated. They aren't, but this suited my plan. I kept my boat about thirty yards from his, waiting for him to give me the chance I wanted. Then he got into a big trout, some distance away, and stood up to play it, as he was in the habit of doing. Quickly, I lifted the salmon rod from its sleeve and began to paddle closer to where Bill was fighting his fish. He was too busy to notice, with his back turned.

I stood up and made a few air casts to get the range and then, just when Bill was bringing in his fish and reaching for his landing net, I cast over his shoulder. The little grapnel snagged the rough tweed and at once I whipped up the head of my rod.

His feet were squarely planted, but the unexpected pull of my line, although quite gentle, caught him off balance, and he dropped rod and net and fell backwards into the green water.

I took up the slack and then, unwrapping the anchor, hooked it on to the line so that it rode down out of sight to where it would begin to pull Bill downwards into the depths. I braked the reel and watched, fascinated, as the line tautened across the gunwale. He would never hurt Rosie again, I thought. Soon, I could fish him up and remove the hooks, leaving no evidence whatever of what had happened.

Suddenly, to my horror, the line slackened. Frenziedly I pulled at it, but there was nothing on it. The anchor had come loose. I guessed what had released it. It was made of rough galvanized iron and its heavy weight, moving fast down the line, had snapped it, releasing Bill from its dragging hold. Desperately, I looked across at the other boat, to which mine was still drifting.

My heart seemed to stop. It's true to say that the hair on my neck stirred in fright. There were knuckles grasping the farther gunwale.

I paddled closer and rounded the end of the boat. Bill's head was just out of the water, and he was gasping for breath, making raucous noises in his throat. He had no strength left.

But I couldn't finish him off. Planning a murder, I found, is one thing; pushing a drowning man's head under the water is quite another. I got into his boat, thrust my hands under his armpits, and hauled. He came over the side like a stranded whale and lay on his face—which was just as well, for clearly visible on the shoulder of his coat was my little grapnel, with the line trailing back into the water. I snipped it off, leaving the hooks, and got to work on Bill, stripping off his jacket, which I bundled up, and wrapping my own coat around his shivering body. "That'll keep the chill out," I said encouragingly. "Just lie still." I began to press down on his back, rhythmically, and more water came out of him. He was now breathing more easily.

I transferred my gear to Bill's boat and rowed it to the shore, leaving the other boat to be picked up later. I stuffed the wet jacket, with the telltale hooks, into the car boot, saying I didn't want it to drip on my upholstery.

On the way home Bill started to stammer his thanks. "I c-can't explain it," he said. "It was as if I was tugged backwards. I went in deep and it took me an age to get back to the surface. If you hadn't seen it happen I'd have been a goner. I couldn't have hung on any longer. But I still can't—"

"You were overexcited, fighting that bloody great trout. I've always told you to play them sitting down."

"I really can't thank you enough," he said between chattering teeth. "And Rosie . . ."

I was silent for a moment. "You ought to treat her a bit more carefully, Bill. She's rather fragile, you know."

To my amazement he began to laugh. "That's a good one," he said hoarsely. "*Fragile*! Our Rosie is a tough little lady, Ray, make no mistake."

"There was no need to give her a black eye," I said curtly.

"Don't talk crap," he said indignantly. "She walked into the bathroom door. I saw her do it."

I didn't believe him. "And those bruises on her arms?"

Now he was getting angry. "Look here, Ray. You've no call to talk like that. You know I'd never hurt Rosie. It was at her gym class, apparently. The instructor—quite unintentional, of course. What's got into you? You know I love Rosie. Even if she does see more of some people than I'd like."

"What are you talking about?"

He stared at the road ahead. "Sorry. I shouldn't have said that. She's promised to go steady in future. In my position I simply can't afford any scandal . . . but of course it's not just that. I won't share her with anybody."

I was too flabbergasted to speak, and just then we arrived at Bill's house. We were two hours earlier than Rosie would have expected us, but I hoped she was in, to look after Bill.

She was in all right.

Bill opened the door and I went through to the kitchen, to put on a kettle. I heard him calling her, and a moment later, as I came into the hall, Rosie was descending the stairs, wearing a dressing gown.

"Are you all right, darling?" asked Bill anxiously.

"Just a headache. I've been lying down. Why are you so early?"

"You'll laugh at this, my sweet. I fell into the lake. But Ray fished me out, bless him. I'll just go up and get out of these things."

She said quickly, "Don't go upstairs, Bill. I'll fetch what you—"

"No good, darling. I'm wet all through." He gently pushed her aside and went up the stairs. Rosie gave me one horrified glance, and put her head in her hands.

Above us there was some shouting and scuffling, and the distinct sound of a blow. Gavin came down the stairs, buttoning up his shirt. He went to Rosie and put his arm round her. "I'm sorry I had to hit him, love, but he was going berserk. You'd better come to my place."

"No," she said flatly.

"What on earth's going on?" I asked, foolishly enough.

They stood there with their eyes on the ground, very young, looking like children caught stealing jam, but their faces still wore an afterglow. I could scarcely speak for disgust. "You told me a pack of lies," I said thickly.

Bill was coming downstairs, his hand to his face.

"Answer me," I said to Rosie.

She raised her head and looked up at me appealingly. "I couldn't tell how I got those bruises, could I?" she said simply. "Gavin didn't mean to hurt me. I *couldn't* tell you the truth, darling."

"I'll show you the truth," I said savagely, and grabbed her hand. (What did anything matter now?) Before Gavin could intervene I'd dragged her through the door and down the path to my car. I opened the boot and showed her Bill's coat, with the deadly little hooks half hidden by the tweed. Then, in a few brutal words, I told her what I had done.

Her face froze in horror and her lips trembled uncontrollably. Then, without a word, she broke away from me violently. Gavin was coming down the path, but she rushed past him and flung her arms around Bill's neck. "Oh, my darling," she sobbed. "Thank God you're safe. I'm such a fool. I do need you so."

Gavin watched this scene, shaking his head, baffled. I don't think he understands women any better than I do. He walked quietly away without turning his head.

He didn't turn up at the shop the following day. But Bill did—to thank me. "I don't know what you said to her, Ray. She won't tell me. But it worked wonders. We'll be all right now, I think. She's very young. She can't help it when men fall in love with her." He insisted on shaking my hand. "I owe you an awful lot, Ray."

In a manner of speaking, I suppose he does. But it's all a bit odd, isn't it?

REMEMBER MRS FITZ

George Sims

DEAR BARBARA BENYON,

I expect you have already peeked to see who this letter is from. Ha-ha! That was no good as you do not know me and I shall not put my given name but the one assigned to me from The Other Side. Yes, 'tis true, I am only an admirer from afar, but I do know quite a lot about you. For instance that you work at Barclays Bank in the Strand branch—in fact it was to Messrs Barclays that I was first indebted for your name, Miss Barbara J. Benyon, on that plaque which you so dexterously and prettily place on the counter.

But I am not one of your customers—I was only in the Strand branch on an errand or "a chore" as Mother used to say—so that will stop you puzzling as to which one I might be. What else do I know about you? Well, that you travel to and from the bank on the number eleven bus and that you sometimes have lunch at Mario's in Agar Street. And occasionally you take sandwiches and eat them in Lincoln's Inn Fields or on the Embankment. Down by the Thames you tend to "moon about" and stare at the famous old river as if it might reveal some of its strange secrets to you, and I do think you are rather "the dreamy, romantic type". You have a tiny gold watch on a pigskin strap which you consult a good deal at lunch time, and a gold locket but no rings I'm glad to say! You are not tall, in fact "Five foot two and eyes of blue". You recently had a summer cold. You read the *Daily Mail* on the bus in the morning and sometimes buy the *Evening News* on leaving the bank. All correct so far? Obviously I know where you live. By the way that girl who shares your flat is definitely not the type I should trust but more of that anon.

As for myself? Well I can't say too much at present but tallish and considered rather good-looking—*if* you like the dark, Romantic type. Perhaps more of a thinker than a man of action but reasonably outgoing with a good sense of humour, affectionate, responsive and above all sensitive! Much travelled and tanned!

I've been told that I'm inclined to be a bit suspicious, someone once said Paranoid (cheek!), and to search out other people's faults but I have not discovered any in you so far. May I be rather personal for a moment and say how much I like some of the frocks and suits you wear to work. But I can't say that I entirely approved of the rather revealing sun-suits you and your red-headed flatmate wore by the Serpentine last Sunday. And the horrid Lewd way she lay, exposing all she had got! She definitely flaunts herself does that one and is obviously obsessed by the evil Serpent SEX. You see it is true, as Mother used to say, that some girls "have no sense of what is proper". They taunt men, lead them on and then are surprised when they end up in trouble! But that's the red-headed Tart's problem, not yours. I see that I've been led away by her disgusting goings-on from saying that in your grey dress, the navy one and the dark brown suit you remind me more than somewhat of my Mother and that is really the reason I have written to you. She had tiny feet like you. She always got her "Boots" as she called them at the fashionable Mayfair shop Pinet which was the only place where she could obtain the extra-narrow size three fitting. I still have a pair of her "Boots" in a special case of which I'll tell you more some time. It is a very special case with three locks and a combination padlock so you can tell the contents must be important.

Well I must sign off now for "time's a-fleetin'"—without of course any hope of a reply. Think of me just as a shadowy background figure, a humble patient sort of chap who does not intend to interfere with your life at all, but to remain watching over you with the very friendliest of intentions. Believe me ever,

Sincerely yours,
Laszlo

Dear Busy Bee,

Who sped away from Barclays Bank at lunch-time today and *not* on her usual stroll to Lincoln's Inn Fields or the Thames? Who

verily raced along the Strand and past the Royal Courts of Justice
(Justice!—that's a joke), then up Chancery Lane? Who had to
jump out of the way of a mad lout in a careering black Bentley?
Who went into Star Yard and entered the gloomy legal premises of
Messrs Castle, Harding & Walker? That's right—Barbara Busy
Bee. And who followed her and waited ever so patiently outside?
Yes—faithful Laszlo. My Mother always told me that Patience
was a great virtue. "Just wait and see, our turn will come," she
used to say. I do hope that there was no very serious reason for you
having to consult those legal codgers. If I had to hazard a guess,
and it is something that I am rather good at, then I should say
trouble at home. By which, of course, I mean trouble with that red-
headed Tart *who takes men to your flat when you are not there*!! Not
that I should dream of interfering there unless, of course, I sensed
you wanted me to. Sometimes we all have to turn at bay!

I've been brooding on this troublesome, indeed worrying
problem of yours despite glares from an ugly, probably disease-
ridden, Keeper in a Park which shall remain nameless. I must say
that it is a shame you have been forced to go to Law to get that Tart
out. "You can't trust the Law," Mother used to say. How right she
proved to be! Patient, clever, resourceful, "a woman of most
unusual qualities" as they admitted in Court, would you believe
that such a woman could *end up dying in a prison cell*?

Yours sincerely,
Laszlo

Dear Barbara Benyon,

Today, rather selfishly I suppose, I want to write about a matter
which does tend to weigh me down a bit. I say selfishly because I
know I should only be concerned with that Scarlet Woman
flatmate who is making your life hell at the moment, and turning
your flat into a noisome pit with her SEX goings-on. But this
personal matter oppresses me somewhat and I just feel I must get
some of it down on paper, set it straight for once and for all.
Obviously you can't reply but I sense that you are *simpatico* and a
trouble shared is a trouble halved. Anyway, see what you think.

A while ago now, I suppose it must be quite some years, against
my father's wishes, I instigated a long series of seances for

communication with the control Black Feather and Mother's mediumship.

The communicators who gave me the messages were the famous old Italian fiddle-maker Stradivarius and the Russian composer Rimsky-Korsakov. Up to that time you have my word for it that no messages from those illustrious gents had been received at our house! Strad, who manifested first, stated at once that he was sending the messages solely for me, and that I must collect them and write them all down, and that the financial results were to be solely for Mother and myself, and mainly for the purpose of assisting me and establishing me in my career. *At hardly any of these seances was my father present*!

Sorry if I have rambled on a bit but you know how it is, things do tend to get bottled up over a period, particularly if you have no one to "chinwag" with, and then it's best just to let off steam. Anyway, thanks again for listening.

Sincerely yours,
Laszlo

Dear Barbara Benyon,

Today I was very touched to see you looking pale and cast down with care—all because of the terrible troubles that the red-headed whore has brought upon you. She is definitely SEX mad—I know the type!

Of course I noticed that you did not go out with her this Sunday even though the sun was baking hot. Very wise. Take my tip and keep away from her as much as possible until the creaking, slow-grinding Law at last compels her to leave your flat! I noted by the way that she has now got some oily-looking chap, probably her Pimp, to accompany her to and from work. But her time will come so please do try and cheer up. Forget her and that will undoubtedly bring the roses back into your cheeks.

Sincerely yours,
Laszlo

Dear Barbara Benyon,

Only me! Yes, verily, I am doubly blessed. Fortunate indeed to have the famous Black Feather as my control—yes, you're right, the very same Black Feather who was once "left-hand control" for the illustrious Madame Eusapia Palladino. And dear old Strad who manifests so readily, really "at the drop of a hat". Rimsky is much more difficult I'm afraid, and sometimes seems to be sulking, but I suppose he is still much tied up with music matters on The Other Side.

Barbara—we are both, there's no point in being falsely modest, generously endowed with blessings. However I do sometimes wonder if you may not be the type who accepts same without much thought for others less fortunate.

A friend of mine is a case in point. He happens to be smallish. For that reason he had to take humble employment—definitely not in keeping with his education, upbringing, family background, etc. This friend of mine was always most methodical, patient and anxious to please. But the men in the place where he worked were immediately jealous of him and could see that the Boss took a friendly interest in him and that he was well placed for early promotion. So they started a campaign! Threats, hints, lies and abuse! They tried a number of plots which all failed miserably. Vile libels, etc! The last straw was the planting of stolen goods! A fiendish set-up you say? But would you credit that such a chap would get his own back on that foul gang of toughs? Well he did! With Strad's help! They certainly reaped the whirlwind, or should I say the furnace? Ha-ha! I'll tell you all about it one day.

I don't think I ever finished off the tale about The Revd Gent my father. Through a foul trick he published all those confidential chats with Strad and Rimsky on his own!! *This meant the loss of ten years work*! After a lot of wrangling father gave us a signed contract that we should receive fifty per cent of the profits. And a signed confession of his own free will. Strad said that compromise was the only way and I thought we should listen to the wise old fiddle-maker. So, all serene. Then—what do you think? Father decamped, a moonlit flit no less, with that precious contract and confession. Now you may have some inkling of what Mother went through at that precious Vicarage! We of course wrote to the publishers insisting that a clause should be put in the contract to allow us a percentage. Result? No reply.

What a nice new black dress. And I was glad to see the way you ignored that crude oaf who wanted to maul you when getting off the bus this morning. Don't think that we are all like that (SEX mad).

Yours sincerely,
Laszlo

Dear Barbara Benyon,
May a comparative stranger give you a word of advice. Fairly blunt but with the very best of intentions withal. Don't encourage strange men by smiling at them. Now you see how closely I have you under observation.

Yours sincerely,
Laszlo

Dear Barbara Benyon,
Did I ever tell you about Mrs Fitz? Not her real name of course, I'm rather careful about such things. She definitely "took a shine" to me. Of course I could see some of her faults, at least some of the physical ones, from the start. Those great thick legs with ankles that bulged over her size nine plates of meat—it amused her to contrast them with my own very neat size fives. That none too clean neck and oh those hairy moles! But something about her manner, at first she feigned a quiet modesty, reminded me of Mother. Later on I found out her true nature—how greedy she was—and other things!

Mrs Fitz lived all alone like a hermit in a great big dark house, but pigged it in only two rooms, never cleaning anything and hardly ever washing her crocks. It was a very gloomy house with big trees that shut out the light and the garden was all overgrown with weeds. Every single room in the house was full of junk. She never threw anything away and there were hundreds of empty bottles and piles of tins and bags in the kitchen. Another pile of unread newspapers and unopened letters in the hall. There was so much stuff in some rooms that you couldn't get into them. I only hung around there as she promised to set me up in my career.

In a hurry so I must close.

By the way am I mistaken or is someone following you? *I mean someone apart from me of course.*

Sincerely yours,
Laszlo

Dear Barbara Benyon,

"Suffocated with a pillow!" I hear you exclaim your doubt and derision at the very suggestion. Yes, indeed, how could they be sure? Who is to say that The Revd Gent did not suffocate himself? One thing is certain—Mother was quite innocent. But you see Strad says there is no justice in this world. He says that on The Other Side all is different. Sometimes, I must admit, I do rather long to be there.

Ever sincerely,
Laszlo

Dear Miss Benyon,

Just to say that I am definitely on to the blond beast who is now your constant companion and his Jewboy friend. Are the police really recruiting Yids now? Well they must be hard up if they stoop to having Kikes working for them! The police would be well advised to keep out of my affairs. Where do they all skulk when they are really needed?

One tries hard only to think of pleasanter subjects but under pressure it is difficult. Oh yes, I was telling you about Mrs Fitz (not her real name so no investigations about that by request please). Would you believe she had kept all her old toys and those of her long-dead brother? On the sideboard in the dining room there were long lines of toy soldiers smothered in dust. One afternoon she fell asleep, looking a disgusting sight with her large mouth wide open and showing her denture plate. I explored the whole place and decided on a plan.

Feeling rather down and "put upon". However Strad says "not to worry".

Faithfully yours,
Laszlo

Dear Miss Benyon,

Today when you stopped to buy your *Evening News* you were carrying a small parcel. Blond beast was wearing a shoddy blue suit while Jewboy skulked along behind, looking furtive and ashamed of himself. Now you can see you are all closely observed.

At no time did dear old Strad speak to my father!

Shall I give you a clue as to my present whereabouts? A café in the Strand not a million miles from Barclays Bank & Barbara Benyon. I can say that as I shall not come here again. A giant of a pimply waitress flicked some crumbs on me.

Strad has just come through loud and clear. Danger ahead! So I'm off. Your bullies are even worrying Strad now but I don't suppose that bothers you.

Faithfully yours,
Laszlo

Dear Miss Benyon,

We wrote to the publishers on countless occasions in re The Revd Gent and his claims that Strad had first manifested to him.

Had to move in a rush as you undoubtedly gleefully heard and lost all my notes regarding the trial. Also various files of useful information, OFFICIAL DOCUMENTS and other valuable possessions. A savage blow but I keep trying to look on the bright side.

Did I ever tell you about that terrible woman Mrs Fitz? That's what I called her as she thought she was "out of the top drawer" all right. Lording it like Lady Muck. Behaved as if she was made of money but had hardly anything apart from that old house which she could not sell as it was riddled with dry rot. She didn't wash but smothered herself in cheap scent. And the house stank because all the windows were closed and nailed up fast. She was scared stiff of burglars!

Father said that he would have to take legal proceedings. That he was determined to stop us "making his life a misery". We soon settled his hash!

Faithfully,
Laszlo

Miss Benyon,

Not to mince matters your louts are making my life a misery! In a second rush move I lost Mother's precious case! I am definitely being hounded. Not a nice feeling. I have written to the Papers and the Authorities about this sort of thing before but nothing is ever published as they are all in cahoots.

I stake my reputation on the authenticity of Strad's messages. But for say £100 I would have been willing to relinquish all rights. This letter is a jumble because of your loathsome bullies.

Faithfully,
Laszlo

Benyon,

Mrs Fitz was disgusting. I stuck it out there even when she tried to make a fool of me by sitting me on her lap—just like a ventriloquist's dummy. She said she was sincerely interested in The Other Side and promised to help me with my career. And she wanted to act as my medium—as if I would ever use anyone apart from Mother! Finally I realized that all she was interested in really was SEX. So I tied her up when she was sleeping and put a plastic bag over her head to keep her quiet. Then I smashed all the plates in that old sideboard, the tin soldiers, the pictures, the stuffed birds, the paintings, the clocks. I emptied every tin and jar in the kitchen. I made a pile of the filthy curtains and carpets and emptied bottles of ink over them.

But I doubt if she contacted the police. Because she understood that once I'm roused I'm liable to hit back. And then again *I'm very patient and willing to wait for years if need be.*

Strad insists that I "go underground". All this needless anxiety on top of Mother's tragedy. I definitely advise you to call off your hounds. Anyway they are bound to lose interest after a bit if I lie doggo. I know that from experience. Then I shall return. Remember Mrs Fitz!

Ever faithfully,
Laszlo